C000046839

Colin Townsend was born in Wimbledon SW19, but spent most of his upbringing in Norbury and Streatham. He completed an engineering apprenticeship. He then moved to Basingstoke for home and job, where he worked as an engineer for 40 years. He has a son, a daughter and two grandchildren. His partner, Sally, passed away a few years ago. Now retired in New Milton, he leads multiple groups on behalf of 'Walking for Health'.

For my family

Colin Townsend

FLIGHT TO FREEDOM

AUSTIN MACAULEY PUBLISHERS™

LONDON • CAMBRIDGE • NEW YORK • SHARJAH

A CIP catalogue record for this title is available from the British Library.

ISBN 9781398420649 (Paperback)
ISBN 9781398420656 (Hardback)
ISBN 9781398420663 (ePub e-book)

www.austinmacauley.com

First Published 2022
Austin Macauley Publishers Ltd®
1 Canada Square
Canary Wharf
London
E14 5AA

Flight to Freedom

He grabbed her quickly and pulled her near to the door and using the keys, he unlocked the hand and ankle cuffs that secured her. She sighed so he did not need to check her pulse but managed to lift her onto his shoulder. He noticed how light she was, a bonus in a way, as he managed to move quickly across the road, he quickly retrieved his bow and disappeared into the bushes, he managed tripping only twice and then not enough to floor him.

~~~o~~~

The coffee shop had recently been re-decorated and although the standard of coffee hadn't changed, thank goodness, all the equipment had been brought up to date; there were comfortable seats and sofas around the sides of the lounge. The décor was a light coffee colour, sort of latte with darker wood panelling and the pictures were of coffee-related scenes, and of the different coffees they made. There was also a glass cabinet with cakes and biscuits, and another one with an assortment of different flavoured sandwiches on offer. The tables that used to rock badly on uneven legs, spilling the coffee when customers seated themselves had been replaced, saving the customers the hassle of folding up paper napkins to push underneath to steady them. It made typing easier on the laptops most carried. There were more electrical points for charging batteries and connections for charging phones as well. The WiFi code was displayed clearly to see as on a lot of European cafés, all was done to facilitate the use of the premises by students and professionals who seemed to use it as an impromptu office.

It had become one of the main meeting places around town for some of them, during the day and in the evening; not everyone wished to meet at the pub.

The three girls: Isabella, Jenny and Deb sat in the coffee shop drinking and chatting. Although the girls all attended the same university, they were all studying different subjects so could only meet once a week.

Deb was studying English, she stood about 5 feet 8 inches with raven hair, brown eyes and naturally dusky complexion and of slight stature. Deb had always been practical, friendly and mixed easily. She was lodging with six others in a converted house, not great but comfortable now that she had been there over two years, and as all were doing the same or similar courses, they could and did help each other out.

Jenny was taking Physics standing 5 feet 5 inches tall with blonde hair, striking green eyes, fair complexion and a bit of a dreamer, she loved her subject; staying with four others in her lodgings, amiable in her disposition but with a good sense of humour. The Physics department was at the other end of the city to the rest of the University, so she was a distance away from the others. Isabella was 5 feet 6 inches, blonde with outstanding hazel eyes and a complexion to match; she was studying Modern History. Her accommodation was back at Halls for her last year, so she was paying a little less than the others, but was also with other History students. Bit of a joker whenever she got the chance and liked to chat.

All in all, the three suited each other and moulded into a tight-knit group; they enjoyed each other's company, had a laugh and agreed on a lot more than they didn't. Living not too far from each other helped, as they could travel together, well some of the way anyway.

They had part-time jobs both to help pay the costs of being at university but also to save some money up for the year they intended to stay away for. They had met originally when in their first year staying in the same Halls.

Contrary to belief, they didn't spend the evenings drinking and generally enjoying themselves, they were all dedicated in the subjects they had chosen and would spend most evenings deep in revision. Often working till the early hours. They all realised that to get a good grade at the end of the courses they had chosen was far from easy.

They were planning the adventure of a lifetime, a backpacking tour for a year away from home. The trip was being planned for when they finished their degrees in the future. They felt that they had earned it, and would only have this one chance to see some of these places before starting work in earnest.

They all had paper and pens to hand as well as laptop computers which were part of the necessary accoutrements that they carried as undergraduates.

The planning for this trip of a lifetime had to be meticulous but be flexible in regard to altering locations if necessary. They all knew that this long trip would cause their parents a great deal of worry whilst away. They would understand, they hoped, because this would be a once in a lifetime chance to see much of the world before settling down and beginning a career.

They got back to sorting the trip out.

"Right", said Isabella, "let's start with the date that we want to leave on – a weekday will probably be the cheapest."

"Yes, before the school holidays when everything goes sky high," Jenny agreed.

They all opened up the diaries on their laptops and a date was soon agreed by them all.

They had already agreed whilst chatting previously that they would visit at least three continents. Africa, Asia and Australasia. Also exploring parts of Europe, the continent of which the UK was geographically at least a part of. Jenny suggested that they should ink in the definite parts of the journey that were on all of their wish lists, having already agreed on some of them. All wished to spend a large proportion of the time away in Australia and New Zealand.

Deb suggested that it would be good if they could be there for at least half of their time – many students had travelled through Australia and New Zealand and had been there for a full year and thoroughly enjoyed it. She would like to be there for at least six months and all agreed with that. It was considered to be the safest country to visit.

It was well known that it had a superstructure for backpackers; it had become an industry there. The people there were renowned for their humour, helpfulness and the country was massive. It had so many different climates and places to see, and of course, there was the magnificent 'Great Barrier Reef', so six months was not really enough time to do it any kind of justice.

That left Europe, Africa and Asia.

Isabella suggested that they look at spending two months in each continent and work around that time frame. "To start with, but bear in mind that Europe is going to be the cheapest and easiest place to visit when we are at work. So we should probably spend less time there now."

Isabella said, "Let's work it out from the start of our journey, listing the places or cities we wish to see."

"I would like to spend some time in Paris, as there's so much to see there, the Eiffel Tower, the Louvre, and lots more," said Jenny.

"Is there anywhere else we would go to on our way through France, or do we just head across towards Italy."

"I'd like to go to Barcelona in Spain as I heard from previous backpackers that there is a fruit farm there that is a good payer with good facilities for pickers, we need to earn money as we go or we won't get very far. There is unlikely to be anywhere in Africa we will get work."

"Mmm, yeah, the weather should be nice and warm and it's near the sea as well, isn't it? I'd like to visit Italy, Rome, we really need to go there," Deb enthused.

"Hang on!" said Jenny looking at the map she had open in front of her, "we need to travel in a logical route, we don't want to travel to the same place twice. Look at the rail routes, whether we travel by train or coach they tend to use the same city routes. If we go to Barcelona from Paris, we bi-pass Italy. We need to go from Paris to Rome.

"There is student backpacker accommodation available across all these countries.

"Looking at the rail routes, we could then go from Italy to Barcelona."

Isabella pointed out that they needed to get from Europe to Africa, so they needed to finish in a city with international links to the African country they were intending to visit next.

There were many countries in Africa that were dangerous to visit so they had to research a route via the UK home office reports. After some debate using maps and the home office reports, it was decided to cross to Africa from Lisbon. This would be the safest and cheapest way. They would land at Berithroa and be able to use the railway to get to Johannesburg in South Africa.

When they got to South Africa they could see the nature reserves, maybe go on a safari, see the indigenous animals, lions, elephants and rhinos in the wild perhaps.

They would then be able to travel from there to Bangkok in Thailand which also had a lot to see and from there on to Australia.

That pretty well sorted out the route they would take, but the logistics and bookings would take a while longer. It was decided that each girl would organise part of the journey and as long as they all agreed with it they could reconvene in a week's time at the coffee shop.

Their planned route was worked out so it would be:

UK to Paris France

France to Rome, Italy

Rome to Barcelona, Spain

Barcelona to Lisbon, Portugal

Lisbon to Berithroa

Berithroa to Johannesburg, South Africa

Johannesburg to Bangkok, Thailand

Thailand to Malaysia

Malaysia to Australia

They had been told by other students that the best way to get around Europe easily and cheaply was to get a rail pass. They went to their laptops and looked up the prices. By purchasing these train passes they were able to use the different country train networks as they wished.

They had to work out how long they wanted the passes to last for and they could get to Paris using the Eurostar Train from London through the Channel Tunnel all on this pass.

"Let's leave how long we need to be there till next time we meet," said Deb, "they are cleaning the tables, and we are stopping them closing, they are going to ask us to go soon."

The others agreed and they went back to the different living quarters which they shared with students on the same or similar courses to their own, quite satisfied with what they had sorted out.

It had been a week and each girl had tried to sort out different parts of the journey. Each had e-mailed their parts to each other so that when they met they would be in a position to finalise much more of the trip.

It was Isabella's turn to get the coffees, Deb and Jenny had flat whites, hers was a cappuccino. She carried them over to where the others had taken a table with comfortable seats.

"How are you all doing? Is everything going okay this week?" asked Isabella, sitting down.

"It's been a bit hard this week but getting there now, so hopefully everything's back on track but we'll wait and see," Deb replied.

"Here's your coffee," said Isabella.

It's getting a bit intense, all the revision mixed in with studying to write the dissertation that was their final trial; this had to be presented to both the examiners and the rest of the students in their year, to that end they had to rehearse giving the presentation in the auditorium.

It was driving them mad but hopefully, they were close to finishing now.

"Shall we get started then, where were we?" said Isabella.

"Right, how long are we going to stay in Europe? There's lots to see and we want to see the important places that we've already spoken about and some more that we haven't so now we need to finalise exactly what we want to see. Then we can work out how long we are staying in each country.

"We don't have to be exact with our train tickets, we can book a certain date but if we want, we can alter that on the day.

"We must be at the airport in Lisbon for our flight to Berithroa, that we won't be able to alter, so once we book that, we will have something concrete to work towards."

"Right," said Deb, "let's list which attractions we want or need to see."

"France?"

"Champs Elysees, Eiffel Tower, Arc de Triomphe, Louvre and Montmartre," Isabella replied.

"Italy?" Isabella added, "then Colosseum."

"Colosseum, Palatine Hill, The Forum, Trevi fountain, Vatican and Sistine Chapel, St Peters Square."

"We then need to work and get some money together, so it's off to …Barcelona," Deb confirmed.

We need to book our tickets from Lisbon to Berithroa. We then get a train to South Africa and spend a couple of weeks around Johannesburg, go on Safari that sort of thing and then we'll move on across to Thailand spend a bit longer there as it's supposed to be phenomenal. We then travel down to Malaysia and Singapore, spend a couple of weeks there and then we'll get across to Australia and spend the rest of our time away out there. We can be a bit flexible as to when we go across to New Zealand and how long we're going to stay there, just play it by ear, then carry on across Australia until it's time to come home. I don't know whether we need to book that, I suppose we could, but we don't want to tie ourselves down too much, but we must leave before our visas expire as I am certain we will need to get one.

We have to get passes to miss the ticket offices at all the places of interest we're going too, that will save us a lot of time in Europe.

We need to work out whether we need visas as well to go to some countries. Also what medical supplies we need to take, which inoculations we need and what we need to pack. We also need to sort out what sort of backpack we need to get. We will be walking with it for a year and need to put all our stuff in it, so it's got to be comfortable and hard-wearing."

They looked through brochures and found one where the top part unzipped and they could use it as hand luggage. It was a good make so they ordered one each online; it was expensive but worth it.

It would seem that Australia and Thailand were particularly geared up for student treks with everything in place. They both had infrastructures to accommodate this, a whole industry had grown to suit as it was a large money-maker, and so was well organised and relatively inexpensive for the users and added to that extremely safe for backpackers. But after talking to students that had already done this, it was discovered that as everything was already in place, the cheapest way was to just get a visa, get the necessary jabs and malaria tablets and not worry too much about where to go next till they got there, just make an itinerary up but not keep rigidly to it.

It was agreed that they would split the tour into parts, the biggest being Australia, this would appease their parents a bit. There was the advantage there that students were allowed to work their way across the country. The fruit crop picking depended on this. Work in exchange for a small amount of cash, and free accommodation and food.

They looked on the National Health web site to see which inoculations they needed for all the countries. They knew they would need malaria tablets, but also jabs for: yellow fever, Tetanus, Hepatitis A, Hepatitis B and Blackwater Fever.

They could get the jabs from the local hospital for a small charge, but it would be best if they had them soon after finishing the exams. They didn't want any problems over the exam period. But wanted them well before travelling.

They also discovered that they needed visas for Australia and Berithroa, but that it could all be done on the internet, so sooner rather than later.

"I don't think we need to plan anymore, we can just move from the places in Europe as and when we want to," said Deb, "Let's leave it at that."

They all agreed. "We'll book everything we need to and get the visas sorted nearer the date, and tickets for flight and train in a couple of months."

Time passed quickly as they were not only swatting for the exams but trying to sort out the things needed for the trip.

Revision was both monotonous and boring, but to get a good final grade it had to be concentrated on.

Time after time they practised answering questions from previous exam papers, they limited their meetings to one or two a week as they put all their time into swotting for the dreaded final examination and long dissertation.

They all managed to fill in the complex forms for the visas and received them in the post.

Deb and Isabella hadn't said anything to their parents and had decided to spring it on them when the exams were over. Jenny on the other hand had told her parents what was happening all the way through, and they were supportive and helped where they could.

The exams came and went and on the final day, they all met, not in the coffee bar but in a pub in town to celebrate finishing. It would be a while until they got the results, but they were all going home for a couple of weeks before they met up at the station to begin the adventure. They would know their grades before they left.

It was a quick meeting to go through their arrangements and as soon as they had done that, they moved to another bar and partied in earnest.

~~~o~~~

It had been a normal Friday at work for Mike, normal breakdowns on machinery requiring his attention, he had done all his morning checks, testing of alarms, steam checks on the two large boilers that supplied the heat to much of the equipment. Checked the oil in the compressors which supplied compressed air around the factory at 100psi when he had been called to attend the personnel department meeting at 10:00 a.m. not sure why he had been called. Oh yes, it was now human resources; why the change of name he wondered, same job but it seemed to mean less care for the workforce and more discipline. Advising managers and supervising them on how to discipline and sack people rather than help them solve problems.

He was shown straight into the manager's office and saw straight away his own manager was there but could not make eye contact with him. He felt a cold dread and knew that this was not going to be good. The personnel manager whom he had known for a long time was apologetic when explaining that his working for the company had finished and that he was to be made redundant, the money they said he would get was to him large, but he was in shock, and he didn't really hear or understand what was being said to him.

They explained that he must not talk to anyone about the financial package, and even had to use a solicitor to go through the paperwork and okay it at the firm's expense of course.

They said that he would finish on the last Friday of the month.

"Go and get changed and leave the premises, and come back at 10:00 am on Wednesday. That will give you some time to get to grips with it. I know it's a lot to get your head around. You need to sort things out with your solicitor as quickly as possible, so make that your first concern.

"Have a think of any questions you have for us, and we will talk again when you come back in."

"Am I the only one?"

"No, but I can't say any more."

"Okay. Thanks, I think?"

He walked back to his locker and got changed, put his jacket on, walked out to the car park and climbed into his car. He drove out of the security gate. He drove to a quiet place that he had used before. It was an old church car park. He sat for a while to take everything in; he was shocked, saddened and worried. He stopped turned off his engine and phoned his solicitor managing to make an appointment for the following Tuesday morning.

He re-started the engine and drove out to Silchester where the Roman town of Calleva once stood and a high Roman wall still stood. Normally, he would have enjoyed a walk around the site, but today he just sat in his car and thought about things. He felt like crying but managed to hold back. It was not a good time to lose a job, but then he would have to sort something out. If he could get a job, then the money would be a significant bonus for him.

Returning home, Veronica knew there was something wrong as soon as he walked in the door.

"What's the matter?" She asked as he slumped into a chair.

"Bad news at work," he said putting his head in his hands.

"Been made redundant," he said and gave her the paperwork. "Never thought it would happen to me, but suppose it could be anyone and suppose my age is against me too.

"What am I going to do now?"

Veronica sat in silence for a while and read and reread the paperwork.

She got up and walked around behind him, putting her hands on his shoulders and kissed him on the top of his head.

"Bit of shock," she said, "but we need to sort out what to do now, you've got to see a solicitor, so presumably he will be able to give you some advice, but we've always managed to get by and sort things out ourselves. We need to look at this without emotion and take steps to rearrange our lives."

Mike smiled at her, "You're right as always, let's forget it tonight and relax with a few drinks. Tomorrow's a new day and a weekend so not a lot we can do so ideal time to look at things."

"Yes," she said, "makes a change for you to be home at the weekend anyway."

It was the early hours of Saturday when he woke up sweating, the sheets sticking to him. He got up and went into the bathroom. The house was in darkness, but the silence was deafening. They had made him redundant, he was on the scrap heap. He was too old at 48 to get a new job easily, and not old enough to consider retirement. So many financial commitments and worst of all no one to talk to about it and no one to laugh, joke and work with. As with most workplaces in the UK, any problems were discussed and sorted out between mates over a cup of coffee or whatever, this could range from marital problems, pension, financial advice or anything else.

He had always been sociable; enjoying a practical sense of humour with like-minded friends, and now he had nothing. Things always looked darkest in the middle of the night, perhaps it would be better when they had sorted their finances, at least he and Veronica would be able to try to plan things out.

Eventually, his mind was cleared sufficiently to get back to sleep. He hoped that he hadn't disturbed Veronica.

Waking with a start he looked at the clock, it was 8:00 and he normally started at six and had thought himself late. He worked most weekends to give him more money, but it never seemed enough to reach his savings account. His son and daughter relied on him to pay for their needs at university, and he never minded paying in the hope of securing them a good job with better money and prospects than he had. Especially now.

He thought back!

Years ago, the job had been a godsend. It had afforded him a nice house, good workmates and financial stability. He had never been out of work since he left school. He had always enjoyed his work, sure there was the mundane every day chores, but he also found the time to think of new or better ways of accomplishing problems and processes. The work was heavy duty and smelly and it had taken him a long time to get used to the smell in particular. People entering the factory now could not work out how the workforce could stay in such a smelly environment processing meat, and vegetables, but the results were not for consumption, but for pharmaceutical use and you did get used to the smell, well mostly.

The ingredients came in by the ton, but after intensive processing left in small containers weighing a few kilos.

He had worked there for over 25 years and knew nearly everyone on the factory floor.

To clear his head, he changed into his shorts and t-shirt and set off on a walk, the morning was sunny and clear and being the beginning of spring, it wasn't particularly warm, but the leaves were beginning to show on the trees and the primroses were out in force. He left the road and walked through a farm where cows lounged in the spring sunshine. Reaching the lane at the end, he went up and down the hills crossing the main road twice in his circuit revelling in the peace and quiet. He was in no hurry today, the peace and beauty being more important than the speed.

Returning home he stripped off his clothes and jumped into the power shower washing quickly then joining Veronica for breakfast.

Both of the children had nearly finished university and were working part-time to pay for their degree courses. So he supposed that things might be on the up as far as that was concerned.

Something had to come up, whether it be here or maybe abroad, any job would do for the present, but it needed to be found straight away. He needed to get home, sort his CV out and then put it out on the internet, at least he wasn't going to finish working till three and a half weeks' time so that would help. Give him a small breathing space.

Trouble was that everything had changed, when he had finished his apprenticeship. All a guy had to do was walk in the door if you heard of a vacancy, talk to the manager and be hired straight away; no CVs then interviews and if you were lucky, start in a couple of months.

He had always had the ambition to start his own business, perhaps this was the time.

He made himself a cup of tea and sat down in front of his computer. The initial shock had worn off and he was able to focus on the things he needed to do. First on his list was to look at jobs available that might suit him, and he found that there were a few, he wouldn't get as much as he had been, but he had been there for a while.

What sort of business could he start? What could he offer?

A while ago a friend had given him a copy of a CV and a covering letter for sending to companies he wished to join. He was not really serious in trying for another job but had been considerably surprised to get interviews everytime he had used it. The friend had come from the Royal Air Force and had been shown by experts on how to write one.

He updated his CV.

Between Veronica and him, they found all the documents they could find that they might need. Bank statements, bills, his qualifications wage slips for both him and Veronica who worked as a packing supervisor.

They decided to keep the bombshell away from Deb and Jack; they didn't want their change of circumstances to affect them.

~~~o~~~

The families met up at London St Pancras Station to see the girls off. They said they're goodbyes at the barrier as that was as far as they could go without tickets.

So with the usual traditional words ringing in their ears, 'Ring home when you get there', 'Ring every day or so, stay safe', 'Keep your bag close', they went through the barrier and waved goodbye to their families. The trip had begun.

They boarded the train and put their bags in the racks above the seats. No sooner had they made themselves comfortable than the train began to move. It sped through the countryside like a rocket.

"I read somewhere that it reaches about 185mph," said Jen.

It seemed like in no time at all that they reached Paris. They swapped the train for the metro, which they took to their accommodation which was a hostel they had been recommended to at St. Olives Gare Du Nord. They put their bags in the room and had a look around. There was a restaurant and bar downstairs and the prices were very reasonable.

Having had a look around the grounds, they strolled around the streets to take in the atmosphere which was very busy although they didn't have that much time before having something to eat and getting ready for bed to allow them an early start to start to explore the next morning. They already knew where they were going but they wanted to look at their maps again to check how they were going to get on the metro; they knew they only had a few days to sort it all out and wanted to make the most of it.

The first stop was to be the Champs-Elysées, a Paris must-see, an iconic two-kilometre Avenue between the Place de la Concorde and the Arc de Triomphe. Like the Eiffel Tower, the avenue is a symbol of Paris. It is lined with the most prestigious shops and restaurants. The three girls marvelled at the shops and stopped in wonder at the prices. How anyone could afford to buy anything here was beyond them. At the end of the Avenue was the famous Arc de Triomphe which was built by the order of Napoleon and houses the tomb of the Unknown Warrior, where they climbed to the top for a spectacular view of Paris. It took some time for them to get some breath back to enjoy it and take photos, but coming down would be easier. They then went back to the metro so that they could get to Abbesses, the nearest station to Montmartre, otherwise known as the mountain of Martyrs.

The streets where the likes of Picasso walked with many restaurants and coffee houses. They sat down outside of one and ordered and drank coffee. Then having finished sightseeing for the day, they went back to the lodgings and after eating, relaxed outside with a glass of wine and went over what they had seen that day.

Next day, bright and early, they set off to the metro. Today they were going to the Eiffel Tower and the Louvre. First was the Tower, having bought their tickets in advance to get all the way to the top they avoided the endless queues for tickets. The panoramic views of the city were phenomenal from the summit, and they all agreed it was the highlight of the Paris experience despite the queues to get on the lift, but they used the stairs to come back to earth and needed a coffee to re-energise them.

They made their way back to the metro and went along to Rivolli station for the Louvre. They all recognised the iconic Glass Pyramid entrance to the Louvre, that alone was worth seeing. They were also fortunate to be able to see the De Vinci Exhibition, even the building was eight hundred years old which added to the ambience.

There was so much to see, and the place so vast they all decided that they would return as this visit had only been a brief insight as to what was there.

They returned to their lodgings having visited a supermarket to collect ingredients for food and drink for that evening and the long journey they faced early the next morning. It was an early night for them as the train left at 6:40 a.m. and that meant they had to get the metro bright and early with all their bags packed. They were off to Rome.

They couldn't waste time the next morning having to trot down the platform having shown they're tickets, found the seats they had reserved, lifted the baggage into the overhead lockers, sat down and looked around them. The train was wide, tidy and clean; they checked the tickets against the displayed itinerary.

06:40 A.M. PARIS GARE LYON

01:50 P.M. MILANO P GARIBALDI

7h 10m

15:15 P.M. MILANO CENTRALE

18:25 P.M. ROMA TERMINI

3h 10m

They were surprised to see that all seats benefitted from

air conditioning, power outlets, standard leather seats, video entertainment, vending machines available and free WiFi. And some trains even had a cinema car. The train left absolutely on time.

"Bit different from home," said Isabella.

The train passed through the countryside until it reached Milan where it pulled into the station and the girls had a one-hour wait before it carried on to Rome. They decided to stretch their legs for a while and ventured outside the station. It was very busy but having got outside they crossed over the street to a park and strolled around it for a while getting back to their seats with time to spare. They had managed to find a small baker where they purchased some delicious flat breads. The assistant didn't speak English, but they managed to make themselves understood, but when trying to find the cost the girl assistant weighed the items and that gave a price. Cheap too. It gave them something to nibble on for the rest of the journey.

As the train arrived at Rome Station, they could see the Colosseum, and there were many buses and tourist buses driving past the station. The tourist buses were the hop on and hop off type, so they grabbed a brochure to browse later. First priority was to get to the accommodation, which, according to their phones, was only a small walk away. They legged it over and found the small hostel with clean dormitory and kitchen; they had allowed three days to see the sights. Not long, but they imagined that they would be able to access Europe quite easily in the future, so this was really a taster. They bought a bottle of wine and some supplies from a local supermarket, sat at a table outside and ate and drink. They already had entrance tickets which they had bought cheaply online, so all they needed was transport, and Rome had a metro. They decided to walk to the Colosseum which also connected to the Forum and Palatine Hill.

They had been sitting down on the train for most of the day, so decided to go for a walk around the city and explore a bit. Walking through the city, they saw the many shops and cafes all of them busy with both locals and tourists. They window shopped and looked at the wonderful clothing all by well-known designers. As they walked down Via Del Corso, they came to the Trevi Fountain. It was floodlit and looked truly amazing. Each girl threw a coin into the fountain; legend said that anyone who did would return to Rome. It dated back to Roman times and was named after the three streets which is what Trevi means.

"Well, we hadn't intended it, but we have already been to one of the places we intended to see, and worthwhile too, so beautiful with all the statues," said Deb.

The other two agreed.

They stayed a while longer to carry on looking at it, and taking photos but eventually, they made their way back to the lodgings.

The next morning, they enjoyed breakfast together which Jenny made, avocado on toast with poached eggs. A cup of tea later and they were ready to set off on another site seeing expedition.

It took about 25 minutes to get to the Colosseum. They already had entrance tickets which included entrance to Palatine Hill and the Forum, so they went straight in, marvelling at the way it was built as they went. They started with the Arena floor where the gladiators fought with animals and each other.

Then down to the Hypogeum, the underground level where the slaves, prisoners, animals and gladiators were kept before combat.

The third tier is only accessed by joining a tour which would give a good view of the place, but the girls hadn't booked that. There were so many tourists there that the girls never had a chance to talk.

Having left the ruins they went to the forum. Once the centre of public and political life in Ancient Rome, they felt they were walking in the footsteps of the Ancient Romans. This was where the people of Rome had witnessed the funeral of Julius Caesar.

All three of them were impressed with the sights they'd seen.

They came out and sat at a bench and ate the packed lunch they had made earlier. It was already mid-afternoon, and they still wanted to visit Palatine Hill.

Close to the Tiber River, a wonderful green space with wonderful early ruins.

It was 5:30 by the time the girls reached the exit and made for a café for coffee.

They then went back to the lodgings having stopped at the supermarket to stock up for that evening and tomorrow which was the last day of their Rome tour and they would be boarding a train for Barcelona in the afternoon, a 16-hour journey overnight. They hadn't paid for sleeping births but would sleep in the seats. They would undoubtedly get hungry and a cheap cold bag they hoped would pay dividends. So they bought that in the supermarket as well.

They had no intention of a very early start in the morning when they would visit the Vatican. They had their packs with them as they were going straight from there to the station. They walked to the metro and got off at the nearest station. The Vatican, the Pope's residence is a country of its own right and policed by the Swiss Guard. They reached the entrance and saw a massive queue, but their pre-paid tickets got them through at least some of it. The only queues they had to negotiate were for the bag scanners. After a long walk through the museums, they finally reached the Sistine Chapel which took them by surprise as to how big it was and how amazing the decoration was. No words to describe the views, it was far beyond anything they had seen before – it was fantastic.

Having been herded by security through the chapel, they went into St Peters Square. The most impressive part of the square, besides its size, are its 284 columns and 88 pilasters that flank the square in a colonnade of four rows. Above the columns, there are 140 statues of saints. In the centre of the square, the obelisk and the two fountains stood. They carried on being herded until they found themselves at the exit.

"It's good to get out of the crowds," said Jen. "Let's find somewhere quiet and have a cold drink."

"Yes, the Sistine chapel was something else, but the crowds, and security so tight anyone who looked as if they were going to take a picture was pounced on and they herded us along like cattle going for milking."

They had about an hour and a half before needing to get to the station to catch the train so they found a nice quiet café and sat outside and enjoyed cold drinks.

"Well, that's our sightseeing in Rome over," said Isabella. "The thing about sightseeing in Europe is that if there is anywhere we want to return to or have missed, these are the countries we are most likely to get back to. The only trouble is the crowds of tourists; if we do come back, it's got to be at a time when there are far fewer tourists.

"Now we need to cool down and get ourselves prepared for the long journey to Barcelona, where work starts. We've done with sightseeing for a couple of weeks, it's earning some money to carry on with our trip now."

The journey would take about 15 and a half hours, and they had saved money by not booking a sleeping birth, but would hopefully manage some sleep sitting in their chairs. They just hoped there was plenty of room on the train, they didn't want to be packed in like sardines. They would be met at the station by someone from the fruit farm and taken directly to the farm where if rested, they could begin work straight away.

This farm had been recommended to them by other students who told them the accommodation was okay and the food adequate. The pay was according to the weight they picked, they only had to work Monday to Friday, but could work on the weekends if they wanted. They had contacted the farm and had stated they were there for two weeks.

They needed to lift their bank balances, as so far they had only paid for the tourist attractions they had seen and accommodation. Once in Africa, there was little chance of earning anything, so this job was a must. They weren't going to see much of Barcelona, but that was a weekend break from the UK which middle-aged people enjoyed, as far as they were concerned, it was a major shopping area. So they weren't worried about it.

After sitting quietly in the café for a while, they felt fitter and cooler and it was time to make their way to the station and find the train. They found their seats on the train and crammed their bags in the overhead lockers. Deb took out a pack of cards which had kept them occupied over many of the train journeys they had made.

Fortunately, the train wasn't fully booked and they had plenty of room. The train set off on time. After a couple of hours, they dished out the food and drinks, they sat back and enjoyed it. The cool bag had kept it all fresh and the scenery whilst they were eating was beautiful, and they could see the Italian pre alps in the distance. As the train rolled towards Milan, then according to the train map it would pass through Nice, Nemes Avignon then Barcelona, however it wasn't due to stop at any of the stations, just pass through.

They played cards for a while until they were tired, and night closed in. They settled down to sleep, hopefully for most of the journey. At the speed the train was travelling and the darkness outside, there was nothing to see anyway. The days of going to different sights had tired them out, and they were used to train travel so slept through till about 5 a.m. when a trolley service passed them and they had a coffee each. It was only a couple of hours until they reached Barcelona where they were to be met by someone from the farm. They were expected to work that first day. The train pulled into the station at last and the girls who had been looking at the scenery since the train began to slow down on entering the suburbs of the city, prepared to get off.

"Looks good," said Deb, "but we know that this city is renowned mainly for its large and prestigious shops."

The train came to a smooth stop at the platform.

"Time to go," said Isabella, and they stood up to get their bags down. They waited for the rest of the passengers to leave the train then joined them on the platform where they put their kit bags on their shoulders and walked to the exit. As soon as they got to the exit, they saw the minibus with the farm name on it and made their way over, the driver got out smiling.

"I'm Rodrigues," he said, "and the manager of the farm." They introduced themselves and shook hands.

Rodrigues put the baggage in the back and the girls got into the bus and it drove off.

"It's not far; we will be there in about 30 minutes."

As he drove, Rodrigues talked about what they would be doing.

"In the morning, we start early, daybreak, breakfast then work till siesta, 12 noon till 2 p.m. then back to work till evening, then dinner. The contract is five days, but if you wish you can work weekends. Payment is by weight and different fruits have different values so the more you pick the more you get. You are here for two weeks. You will be picking cherries first."

Rodrigues drove off the main road and down a dusty lane to the farm buildings and the accommodation; they found bunks to sleep on and looked at the toilet facilities which were okay including showers.

He left them to unpack and put on overalls for working, as he had explained the fruit juice would inevitably stain their own cloths, he explained that water was always available and they should make certain they were always hydrated. Rodrigues took them into the cherry orchard, the trees were at head height, so no ladders needed and to only pick to the middle of the bush as they would be picking down one side of a cherry corridor, then picking the other side and back on the other side of the corridor. As soon as the basket they were given was full, they had to take it down to the end of the row, leave the full one and pick up a new one. There was music to listen to as they worked which would help.

~~~O~~~

In an office above a restaurant in Madrid sat Miguel Cartelli, relaxed in a comfortable chair in a corner opposite the door, the radio was on and he was reading a newspaper and smoking a cigarette. The office was painted white with cheap but new furniture that was dominated by a desk and chair.

On the desk was a laptop and nine mobile phones, each with a letter identification on it.

This was the main communication set up and the way that the operations being carried out were monitored. All of these phones were burners, untraceable pay as you go phones used seldom and destroyed often, to stop the authorities getting a lead on them.

A central phone which was a different colour was his connection to his superior who could then contact the boss. The system was a safe method of protecting the higher Tiers so that if he was compromised it allowed his contact to close the phone down and isolate the bottom tier. He was expendable.

The peace was interrupted by one of the phones ringing. He put down his paper, stood up and walked across to the desk and sat down again. The phone that was ringing was labelled B for Berithroa.

He picked it up, "Yes!"

No names were ever used.

The voice at the other end spoke.

"There's a possible problem, a contact has told me that there is going to be a crack-down. The narcs have been hassled to put a stop to drugs coming here and getting through to South Africa. The last shipment got through okay but looks like we are going to have a problem next time."

The phone went dead.

The operator used the central phone and took a picture of the phone with the B on it, took out the sim card and smashed it, then removed the phone and smashed that as well, he bagged the pieces so that he could dispose of them later.

He picked up the central phone and opened Facebook. He uploaded the picture he had taken on it and clicked share.

He wrote on paper the message and put it in an envelope, then Miguel returned to his comfortable chair, sat down and carried on reading the paper.

At 2:30, he packed everything up and placing the envelope safely in his jacket pocket he locked up. Walking a few roads down, he came to a building site with boarding surrounding it. He pushed one area and it swung up allowing him access. He walked across to a paved area and lifted the end slab. He placed the envelope under it and put the paving down.

He reversed his steps and went back through the boarding having made sure there was no one about and went home distributing the parts of the broken phone in different drains. His part done.

~~~O~~~

David Martinez walked past the building site and using the boarding let himself in, he stood for a moment and looked about to make sure no-one was watching then went across to the paved area and swiftly lifted the slab removed the envelope and put it in his jacket pocket. He went back to the road keeping his eyes out for watchers and walked to a tram stop where he caught the one to the town centre, Tram Terminus. He changed trams for another going out of town, still keeping a good lookout for anyone watching. Then he went into an office and handed the envelope to a receptionist, turned about and went out again.

The receptionist went to an office door, knocked and entered. One of the three men sitting there nodded to the receptionist to put the envelope on the coffee table. The three men were brothers, and leaders of this drug trafficking gang and formidable criminals. She put it down then went out and closed the door behind her. One of the men took the envelope and opened it, read it and passed it to the next, he read it and passed it to the last one.

None of the three said anything for a while, then they began to discuss it.

"We need to get this sorted quickly, demand for our product is growing and nothing must stop it."

"Yeah, let's use a diversion, plant some gear on someone, and our contacts can make certain that they get caught as a decoy. Then everyone's happy and we can carry on."

These brothers had drug trafficking organized like a well-oiled machine; everything was fixed from the time of ordering, manufacture and delivery. They had made their order well ahead of time so they had a date that the shipment would be made and so could work out the date when delivery had been arranged and how to sort it so that they could put something in place so that people got caught and their couriers could go through with the real shipment.

"We need a date', we've gotta sort out when the actual merchandise is gonna be going through and make sure that everything happens on the same day, that way we should get away with it okay and be able to carry on in the future be tough luck for the people who get caught but too bad," he laughed. "Then we need to sort out a different distribution network for the future."

"Let's do it, we'll get Johan to sort it'. He's pretty reliable', he'll get the job done, we just need to get sorted out with the 'contacts we've got over there'. We can't afford to lose this, it's a big deal and a lot of money is involved."

"Agreed," said the other two.

~~~o~~~

That first day was hard; they collapsed at siesta and just lay there but it seemed like no time at all until they were back at it again and this time until dark. When it was time, they staggered to the refectory where they had dinner which they struggled through and then went straight to bed.

"Be better tomorrow," Deb said, "we'll soon get used to it."

It wasn't better at all and they carried on suffering until the fifth day when they realized that they still had energy enough to chat. Rodrigues came across and sat with them

"You are all doing very well and you are nearly halfway through. Do you want to work over the weekend at all, we are a little bit short of our target, so we are willing to pay an extra 10p a kilo."

The girls had already decided amongst themselves that they would work through. The more they earned, the more they could do later.

Rodrigues was well pleased and explained that his normal pickers and other backpackers wouldn't arrive until the Monday that they left on.

The days merged, there was little to do on the farm and then they had little energy to do anything anyway. At last, they came to the last Friday of their time there. Rodrigues came over, and they knew he was going to ask them about the weekend again and before he could say anything they asked if the 10p extra per kilo still stood and if it did, they would work it.

"Yes," he said, "and on the Monday we will sort out the money we owe you and I will give you a lift back to the station."

On the Monday they enjoyed a late breakfast. After showering and dressing for the journey, Rodrigues came over and thanked them for their hard work and paid them what they were owed and then helped them with their backpacks into the minibus and took them down to the station where he saw them off with a smile, thanking them again.

The train was due to leave at 13:00 and arrive at 6:30 a.m. next day at Lisbon. Yes, another overnight train but they were used to that by now and after an energetic fortnight, sleep hopefully wouldn't be a problem. They would shop for some cheap but appetising food for the journey before boarding. They found a baker where the food looked particularly appealing and bought enough for lunch and dinner, they also managed a coffee to go each and drinks for later.

Again, they boarded the train and made themselves comfortable. The journey was smooth and uneventful, they enjoyed the food then played cards till they were ready to sleep, the seats were comfortable and they relaxed and all slept throughout the rest of the journey. Then they awoke to the train smoothly pulling into the station. They hurriedly placed everything back in their packs and got down onto the platform where they got their breath back and placed the packs on their backs.

They made their way to the first café that was open and had reasonable prices as it was early in the morning. Refreshed and awake, they made their way down to the front of the town looking at the statues which seemed to be entrances to different parts of the town.

They climbed the Hill to Castelo de São Jorge, probably the most emblematic landmark in Lisbon and stands on the summit of South George Hill the highest point in Lisbon and it was nearly time for it to open now. They were pleased with the prices which were cheap and they got student discounts as well. Views from the top of the whole of Lisbon were fantastic, although climbing around on top of the battlements felt precarious without handrails and was quite breath-taking.

They were unable to spend too much time there as they had to get to the airport to catch their flight so they found the exit and began the walk down to the town to catch a tram to the airport. They came across a small bakery making the traditional egg custard tarts which were just being removed from the oven. They ordered a couple each as they were so cheap. They could hardly hold the bag as it was so hot and had to leave them for a while before they could eat them without scalding their mouths. They were delicious! They reached the town where the trams were flying around everywhere. It was a bustling town but clean really clean. Eventually, they found someone who could understand them and told them which tram they needed to catch. Half an hour later, they were standing in front of the airport, a new modern building.

They went inside to book in and get rid of the bags and carry on through into duty free with no baggage to encumber them. But the desks were all closed as the flights were yet to be called as they were very early. The flight times had been changed, they had thought that the flight they were going on was due to depart in about three hours, but it was more like four and a half, so they had to wait, but there were plenty of shops and cafes about to look at but for now they just found a seat to sit down at and get a coffee to go to drink there.

After a while, a couple with their luggage came and sat down near them, and it wasn't long before they were all chatting like old friends. The girls were telling them about their backpacking trip but wanted to look at the shops as many were selling things that were a little bit different. The woman explained that the shops were on two levels and they would need to go downstairs. A sign lit up showing the flight to book in, and it would be open in 45 minutes. The couple sitting with them explained that their flight was not till a bit later so check-in was not open for over an hour yet. But they said if the girls wanted to look at the shops, they could leave there bags with them for a while. The man got up and bought his wife and himself coffee and they got out a packed lunch.

"Okay," said Isabella, "if you don't mind then that would be great."

"Yes," said Jenny, "let's go."

The couple were tucking into their picnic, and said, "Take your time."

And off the girls went with just the top and part of their kit bags which was unzipped so that they could take it as hand luggage as they kept their valuables and passports in them.

They took their time and enjoyed looking around the many shops. When they got back the departure desk was open for their flight, so they collected their bags, thanked the couple for watching over them and joined the queue.

They booked their baggage in, went through passport control through the scanner and into duty free.

~~~o~~~

The couple they had been talking to got up after a while and without haste picked up their baggage and left the airport.

They walked around the duty free until they could find somewhere to sit down relax and enjoy the duty-free hall which was very big with lots of shops to look at, never mind that they couldn't afford to buy anything, it was still nice to look.

They looked at the jewellery and watches tutting at the prices, they tried on the sunglasses and couldn't believe how expensive they were.

A little later, they went over to the departure screen, the display showed their flight was due to board. They made their way through to the seating area for the next procedure for boarding the plane.

Here they had to show their passports and their boarding passes and walked through a corridor and onto the plane where they took their seats in the airplane after placing their backpacks in the overhead lockers above them.

~~~o~~~

Joshua Abebe waited at the front of the queue as he had a priority boarding on the plane that meant that he would be at the rear of the plane taken out using his crutches as he had badly damaged his tendons in his foot but would be out of his cast in a week or so. As he had restricted movement and would get a seat near the aisle so that he could stretch his leg out a bit for a bit more comfort. The cast he had on was a split cast which allowed the leg to expand as, apparently, when flying his leg could swell which could cause him to have a blood clot, they had allowed his wife and children to board with him.

The family made themselves as comfortable as possible and Janet managed to get their hand luggage into the overhead lockers after removing essentials like colouring books and toys. He gave Janet a smile, they had really enjoyed the holiday, but still looked forward to getting home.

The seats were a bit cramped for him being so large at 6 feet 5 inches high and of a wide stature with no fat, but he knew the flight was fairly short and they should have a bit of help at the other end to get home, but they were dreading this flight, would the kids behave.

A short while later, the rest of the passengers came down the aisles, searching for the seating allocated to them and getting comfortable. The flight crew made certain everyone was seat belted properly and prepared for take-off, then did the usual pre-flight emergency drill whilst the plane taxied to its take-off position on the tarmac. The engines revved up and the brakes released and they were pushed back in their seats then all of a sudden it went smooth and they were airborne.

After a few minutes in the air, the seat belt lights came off and they were able to relax. The children had been sitting still for quite a while and were beginning to get a bit restless, some of the passengers were getting annoyed with them. The three girls, however, enjoyed playing with them, and played with them making faces at them and playing peepo and things like that, and Joshua and Janet were very appreciative of that, it made the flight a lot easier. They had been dreading the flight and trying to keep control of the kids, and it was a relief for the kids to get some different entertainment. Instead of tears and tantrums, there was laughter and giggling instead. After about two and a half hours, the plane started to descend and the seatbelt sign came on. Joshua and Janet chatted to the girls, and when they asked him what he had done to his leg, he explained that he had damaged it whilst running and hurdled a small fence. He neglected to tell them his profession or that he had been chasing a thief who when he injured himself could have escaped, but his ever-athletic partner had caught him. It had annoyed him that he had damaged his leg not long before he went on holiday and Janet was definitely not amused.

The plane descended and came into land for its refuelling stop, the passengers weren't allowed off and an hour later it was back in the air. Thing carried on as before with Deb helping one of the children with some painting. There was a bump and they were down and the plane taxied to near the main terminal building. They had to sit patiently whilst the mobile steps were brought out and the doors were opened. The couple and their children, the girls, said their goodbyes as Joshua was a priority and left the plane first. He and his family were helped out of the plane and down the steps, sitting with his leg fairly still meant that it had become a little stiff, but he managed and at the bottom of the steps was a small mobile which whisked him and the family off to the baggage and customs building.

Zane Bello was a sergeant and friend to Lieutenant Abebe and he made his way through the airport customs area to help his friend and family to his car parked outside. No-one stopped him, he just waved his warrant card at them and that was enough. He reached the conveyor where Janet was awaiting their baggage and was ready to strong-arm the cases onto a trolley. He slapped his friend on the back, still taking it easy then he laughed as did Janet.

"Oh," she said, "thank goodness his carer is here, at last, to give me a rest. I thought that I only had two kids, but I suddenly gained another one."

Zane laughed, "I've always found that myself, and I feel like a carer as I have to look after him all the time he's at work."

The baggage was at last on the conveyor, and Zane easily slung it into the trolley and followed them through customs and through to his car. Joshua noticed a bit of a kerfuffle over one side of the customs hall but couldn't make out what was happening and with the kids being a bit wild and he just wanted to get out of the airport and get home, so he didn't take too much notice of it.

Zane helped them into his car which fortunately was large and spacious and there was plenty of room.

"Did you two have a good holiday," asked Zane.

"Yes," Janet said, "great really enjoyed it. Really needed it, now back to work and the kids back to school."

"I'll be back at work I suppose, probably tomorrow," said Joshua, "So I'll see you tomorrow."

Zane gave them a hand into the house then grabbed the kids one under each arm and took them giggling into the house.

~~~o~~~

The three girls went down the steps and onto the bus which took them to the luggage collection point.

Isabella, Jenny and Deb were in good spirits when they went along to the luggage carrousel to retrieve their luggage and having retrieved it, they zipped the parts of their bags back together again and proceeded to customs with passports at the ready, never dreaming there was going to be any problem.

They placed their baggage on a table and the Customs officers gave them cards in their own language asking whether they packed everything themselves and all that sort of thing and warning them it was an offence to lie. It never occurred to them that anyone had tampered with their bags so they just said, "Yes, we did the packing."

Their bags were checked, by turning out everything on to the table then pushing it to the end where they had to repack everything in them. Isabella was a bit dismayed to see all her clothes and belongings scattered across the tables but accepted it was the way, and began to repack.

Deb bag when tipped out contained a plastic bag of white powder which she had never seen before and the customs man held the bag up triumphantly and looked at her and said, "This looks like drugs to me."

They took her away and then they checked the last bag but that too was full of only belongings.

The girls were taken into separate interview rooms They were left sitting in front of desks for about an hour until the Federal Police showed up to talk to them about the drugs.

~~~O~~~

Over at one of the other customs areas, a couple just walked right through without a problem and put their bags which were on trolleys in a waiting car and drove away. A couple of miles down the road at a deserted lay-by they were met by another car and transferred the bags into it. A similar suitcase was transferred to the waiting car that they had arrived in, and it took them to a local hotel to stay for a couple of nights before returning home – their part of the delivery finished.

The car now containing the drugs then drove to the border to South Africa where it was again transferred to a different vehicle checked and carried on through the network of suppliers.

The girls were taken into separate interview rooms. They were left sitting in front of desks for about an hour until the Federal police showed up to talk to them about the drugs.

The drugs were taken away to be checked – they came back as heroin. The Federal police took them to a local hospital where all three were scanned to ensure they were carrying nothing internally. Then they were taken to the main police station and locked away in separate cells for the night.

What followed was an exhausting day of interviewing which left all three girls mentally exhausted, as none of them could account for the drugs being in the bags. This became the norm for them for the next three days, as agents took turns to throw questions at them. In the end, the girls were tired beyond belief, dehydrated and hungry especially, as food and drink were not a priority to these officials. They asked to see a representative from their embassy, which was ignored.

Isabella and Jenny were brought together at last. Although they asked about Deb and where she was, they were ignored, paraded in front of a customs official who flourished documents in front of them. They leaned against each other for support, then, handcuffed together were escorted back to the airport where they were taken to a departure lounge and escorted onto a plane where they were put into seats and the handcuffs removed. The police then left the plane.

A stewardess noticed their distress and brought them some water, but wasn't going to communicate with them too much as they had been brought aboard as prisoners and she had no idea what they had done. Though when they asked where the plane was going she told them it was due to land at Gatwick Airport in the UK.

What a relief.

The passengers filed into the cabin and into their seats; the staff went through the usual procedure of safety instructions as the plane taxied to its take-off position. There weren't many passengers and they were spread out with no one near the girls who were by now paranoid and wondering whether they were bugged or something. They whispered that they would not say anything about how they had been treated or what had happened to Deb until they were back in the UK.

After many hours in the air, the plane landed at Gatwick and the doors opened and the passengers were allowed off. Due to having no money, the girls had only been able to get water over the whole flight.

Unbeknown to the two girls, their baggage had been loaded on to the plane and when the girls still shaken stopped before wondering how they were going to get through customs without passports, Jenny recognised her baggage on the turntable and hauled it off. Isabella then caught sight of hers and also took possession of it. They badly wanted to check their bags out to see if the mobile phones or any money was left, but there was nowhere to do this so they walked to the customs area, they checked the top bag and to their relief, their passports were there and on showing them were allowed straight through to the exit.

They found a quiet corner and set about checking the bags. To their relief, the phones and personal carry bag which contained all the cash they possessed was there which meant they could ring their parents to pick them up and even get something to eat and drink. They went through the exit doors into the outside air, where they sat apart and rang their parents. Both sets of parents had been worried as they had heard nothing from their daughters for several days but without a lot being said both parents were going to rush to pick them up. News that Deb was not with them was worrying but their first priority was to get their own daughters home as quickly as possible.

Isabella's father rang Mike to let him know that all was not well. Mike, of course, wanted to drive over immediately to talk to both girls but was told that he would have to wait until the following afternoon as both girls had been through a torrid time and needed to unwind.

Mike then got an e-mail from the foreign office that Deb had been arrested for drug smuggling and was being held in prison until a court case. He was unable to find out any more as the offices had now closed for enquiries till the next morning.

The news of their daughter's arrest came as a massive shock. Early in the afternoon, Veronica and Mike jumped into their car to pay a visit to Isabella's house where Jen was going to be as well as and to tell the parents what exactly had occurred with the arrest.

They arrived at the house and could see straight away that the girls were still very shaken by the experience so Veronica quickly said that if the girls could just tell them what had happened, they would leave them in peace to rest and recover.

The couple listened as the girls recounted the experience, then thanked them and left. They had just about managed to keep their own emotions in check, which they did till they got out of the village and stopped on a farm track, where they both broke down.

They were distraught, it would be so easy to become despondent thinking that life had thrown them another curveball. To believe fate was against them, to give up and vegetate. No! that wasn't the way, and wouldn't help Deb – they must make the best of things. Mike had to go somewhere quiet, somewhere he could focus his mind, this was Mike's way and Veronica understood that. Whatever they came up with had to happen quickly.

Mike would go somewhere peaceful to sort himself out, it was the way he sorted things out, cleared his head, but where? Box hill, a steep hill in surrey and sit on the slope and work things out. He found himself a notepad and pen got into his car and drove the thirty miles there. Although he had Led Zeppelin and the Who on loudly, it did not distract him from driving and thinking, even though he had decided that he would think about nothing until he arrived at the hill.

It was a sunny day, he parked up and moved down the main slope and settled down on the grass to think about what he would do. He took his pen in hand and began to write down his thoughts, he decided that he would put them down in no particular order.

He would let Jack know at York where he had just taken his finals. Jack, he knew, would have ideas, but it was imperative that he made plans himself.

The first thing they needed to do was look at getting help from the authorities. To this end, they drew up a list.

1. Government
2. Foreign office
3. MP
4. Police
5. Solicitor in the country she was imprisoned in.
6. Newspapers
7. Charitable institutions

Veronica would need to spend a day at least on the phone to all these organisations. At the least, the foreign office should be able to advise them in regard to legal help. Jack would just get frustrated dealing with these places and lose his temper. At least after all this they would know more about the options they had.

He also realised that it would involve relying on other people, and he was not over keen on that either, neither of them was.

If none of these organisations would help then it left him no option. What was the saying, hope for the best, but plan for the worst? This brought him to the other option, Rescue!!!

Veronica set up her phone, computer, paper, pen and pencil on the desk they all used. She made herself coffee, sat down and started work.

She rang the Police commissioner first. She did not think that he could help, but he might give her other bodies who might.

The phone was answered quite quickly by a switchboard and they put her straight through.

She explained the situation, but he said that the police in this country could do nothing and that she should talk to the foreign office. So, no help there, but she hadn't expected any. So, she crossed the police off the list.

Next was the Foreign Office, it was them who had notified Mike about Deb by e-mail so they should be able to help.

It took an age to get through and she asked for the person who had sent the e-mail, and after being put through to different departments, she managed to get him on the phone. She explained who she was. He explained that whilst Deb was being held subject to trial, there was nothing they could or would do. They couldn't interfere with other countries law systems. She managed to get the name of the solicitor who was to represent her. Veronica asked whether she could appoint her own solicitor, but was told, "No, the court provided the solicitor."

She asked if convicted, could Deb serve her sentence in this country, but was told again no.

He explained that the consulate would visit her in prison to ascertain that all was well and the prison conditions were acceptable.

There was no more information he would impart. The conversation had ended.

The Government switchboard could only direct her back to the Foreign Office.

Next, she rang her MP she wasn't any help but said she should talk to the Foreign Office.

None of the charities could help at least until she was convicted.

1. ~~Government~~
2. ~~Foreign office~~
3. ~~MP~~
4. ~~Police~~
5. Solicitor in the country she was imprisoned in.
6. ~~Newspapers~~
7. ~~Charitable institutions~~

That only left the solicitor who was to represent Deb. Veronica made a cup of coffee, then settled down to make the phone call to Berithroa. She realised that this would take a while and a lot of patience.

She actually got through quite quickly and asked for the ministry of justice. After about 20 minutes, she was put through to an official there, and he, fortunately, spoke English. He looked through the paperwork and gave her the name, e-mail address and phone number of the solicitor who was to represent her.

She tried to ring but got nowhere, so she sent an e-mail.

She talked to Mike saying it didn't look good. So, they needed to make other plans.

He realised that money was going to be a very big problem so his redundancy payment could be a godsend. Who or what organisation could he use as a rescue option? Did an organisation exist? How could he get in touch with them?

That meant of course that he might possibly have to do it himself, so he had better learn a little about the country.

He would have to get himself fit, he would have to use a boat and transport over land, some form of vehicle suitable for the conditions. Or possibly just transport across land from another country, one with an International Airport. Who knows?

Veronica decided to look at how quickly she could get over to see her daughter, at least she would be close. With this in mind, she looked to see availability for a flight as soon as possible. Before she did that however she and Mike had to sort out what they could do, whether they would be allowed to visit her where she was. They just didn't know anything.

That evening she got a reply from Bolithia, the solicitor explained that she was being held at the prison and there was no way that they would be able to visit her there. He did, however, give them a date for the trial which was in two and a half months and that would be the only time they could see her.

That confirmed the options to them.

~~~o~~~

He looked at his bike in the garage where it was kept, it was covered in junk, dust and spiders' webs. It took him over an hour just to get it out and into the garden to clean it up. Most of the muck came off fairly easily and the more solid stuff came off soon after. Looking at the debris, he remembered the last time he had used it, it was a charity ride and it had poured down with rain continuously, and coming back he had gone down a particularly muddy track. When he had got home he didn't feel up to cleaning the bike and had left it in the state it was in now, slung in the garage. He had jumped into a hot shower to recover and warm up, it had been in November and was icy cold.

He examined the bike in earnest, the tyres were flat and scraping on the brake blocks, so he couldn't spin the wheels to test for buckling. He returned to the garage with a pump in one hand and a tin of the three in one oil his father had sworn by. Surprisingly, the tyres inflated so he carried on pumping until they were hard when he pinched them. He squirted oil into the moving parts, spindles gears steering, crank, chain etc.

Turning the bike over on its back he was able to spin the wheels by the pedals and was pleased to see that the wheels were relatively true. He turned the bike right way up to check the gears and brakes and changed the gears using the levers on the diagonal tube below the handlebars and then lifted the back wheel and spun the pedals, watching the derailleurs change up-down. He would not be able to test the gears properly until he actually rode it. The brakes seemed okay as well but they needed a test ride down the road as well.

He took the bike out of the house for the first time in an age, it still thrilled him and after checking the gears and brakes, he carried on around the block. The brakes did what they were designed to do, as did the gears, so in all he was fairly happy and couldn't wait to start out on his training rides.

He would need to buy four innertubes, two for now and two spares just in case. After putting the bike away, he went on to his computer and onto a well-known map site to plot out his training route. It must start and end from home and last about 10 miles then he could monitor his fitness by how long it took him to complete it. They had just finished building cycle paths all around the town, so this could be a possibility, but the countryside was much more interesting and fairly free of traffic.

To clear his head, he changed into his cycling gear and set off on an old training ride of his, a circuit of five miles, this used to take him a little under half an hour and after completing it and showering, it left him feeling more contented and better equipped to clear his mind and proved the bike's mechanics.

The following morning was sunny and clear, the beginning of spring; it wasn't particularly warm, but the leaves were beginning to show on the trees and the primroses were out in force. He left the road and cycled through a farm where cows lounged in the spring sunshine. Reaching the lane at the end, he went up and down the hills crossing the main road twice in his circuit revelling in the peace and quiet. He was in no hurry today, the peace and beauty being more important than the speed.

Returning home, he stripped off his cycling clothes and jumped into the power shower washing quickly then joined Veronica for breakfast.

She looked him up and down, "Don't go overdoing it," she said, "that won't do any of us any good."

"I know, but I'm alright, and I need to get fit," he replied.

"All I'm saying is, take it a little easier, you don't need to do everything all at once."

"Honestly, I'm fine but I'm so out of condition."

That evening, he was out again putting on his trainers, shorts and t-shirt, and was out jogging for what seemed like miles, but in fact, was only about one mile or so.

Didn't realise how unfit I was, he thought, *This could take ages so I have to push hard even though Veronica worries, I must keep on training.*

As soon as he got back, he had a shower and drove into the town, parked and went down to the bike shop where he bought the spare inner-tubes he needed and a new helmet, lucky it was open till late.

Early again next morning, he was straight out in the garage, where he fitted the innertubes and took the bike out for a trial ride. First ride up the road, and the steering felt a little tight so he went back and gave it another large dose of oil and out again to see if it was okay. An hour later, he was still cycling and enjoying it, but really tired. He needed yet another shower on finishing.

He worked out his route, he would go out via a local farm, even though it began with a hill it was a pleasant start, this would bring him eventually through to charter alley, to Monk Sherborne, Sherborne St John and home. A total of 12.5 miles.

The following morning he was ready to go. Down the road, through some alleys, across the Roman Road to the farm entrance. The way through was sloping upwards and about half a mile long, so by the time he got to the top his lungs were pumping fit to burst and he wondered where he was going to get his next breath from. He undid his cycle helmet as it felt that this would help him to catch his breath. He nearly threw it off but managed to stop himself, and after a while, he was able to wipe the cold sweat from his brow and neck to carry on cycling. It was downhill into Wooton and his confidence soared, well it tried to anyway.

He had found that by concentrating on the road about 10 feet ahead, he wouldn't know how much further he had to go up a hill, but on the downside he could possibly hit something, so every now and then he took a quick look to make sure there was nothing there.

The road he was on revealed a pyramid in the distance but on drawing near he found that it was the headquarters of a stone preparation and polishing company. He came out of the country road onto the busy A339 and realised quickly that he couldn't travel far along this road, not if he wanted to survive, the massive juggernauts nearly blew him on to the grass verge as they trundled past.

He decided to dismount and get across the road on foot as he wanted to turn right to the small village of Charter Alley rather than attempt it on his bike and be in real danger of being flattened.

There was a gap in the traffic so he ran with his bike across the road. The lane undulated up and down so the quicker he went down, the further he would get up the next hill before he had to pedal. With this in mind, he bent over the handlebars in a stoop to give less wind resistance and better speed.

This seemed to work to an extent, up until the last hill in the road, he was already out of breath when he came to a bend in the road only to discover that the hill carried on and got steeper and 25 yards later he came to a complete stop next to a five-bar gate. Behind it, a couple of black shire horses were watching him and appeared to be grinning at him. He scowled back at them and would have liked to sit down for a rest but if he did he knew he would never get going again, so instead he remounted his bike, admonished the horses which made him feel better and rode on. The horses took mouthfuls of grass and completely ignored him.

He cycled past a couple of cottages and was relieved to see that he was at the top of the hill, and turned right by a church towards Monk Sherborne and he was going downhill again past a closed down pub round a long bend and on to Sherborne St John crossing another busy road. He turned right again at the village and after re-crossing the last major road he had crossed and cycled beside a golf course up to the A339 he crossed it again and was pretty well home and able to jump into the shower. He realised that it was going to take some time to achieve the level of fitness he needed to achieve.

~~~o~~~

The next item on his list was a good bow and arrows. He would need some form of weaponry although he hoped that it wouldn't be needed. He and Jack had been members of a club not so long ago. Jack had been good and could have well been a contender for an England junior place. He had made the cut and been in the Archery GB selection team, however, exams had got in the way and he had made the choice to concentrate completely on them as if he got the university place he wanted then he could take up his archery there.

Mike was not so good but practice made perfect, and he would improve. His bow was a compound version but he could only shoot to any form of accuracy from a maximum of 20 yards.

He browsed manufacturers catalogues, he knew that he would have to get a new bow, a more accurate and lighter one than his present one. He would need to be able to estimate distances accurately, he did not want to kill anybody and only intended to fire if there was no other choice. The bow was really a threat, but if necessary he needed to be accurate. He could get some idea as to which bow he needed, looking on the internet and reading the reviews from other users, but at the end of the day, he needed to try one out on a range.

The next day, he woke early, went for a run, showered and then drove to the nearest archery shop which was about 40 miles away, but he needed to try bows out and talk to a compound archer face to face. An archer that had tried out the latest bows for accuracy, he needed to feel how light it was and whether it was in stock or needed to be ordered.

Jack used a Recurve Bow which is the more accurate version of the old longbow, whereas the Compound Bow that Mike wanted used a pulley system to enable far better accuracy and power, as once the string has been pulled back the weight on the archer's shoulders is a fraction of the pull weight on a recurve, this enables the archer far greater accuracy and allows him to hold his stance for a considerable period to aim before shooting. Also, there can be other aids to accuracy fitted, such as a telescopic sight with a level gauge to ensures the bow is completely vertical.

He parked in the car park and went to the counter and asked a member of staff for the best person to give advice on compound bows

He had looked in the catalogue and thought that the Hoyt Pro Edge Elite XT2000 looked good, but he needed confirmation he had read all the specifications and they came out as fast, sleek and pinpoint accurate with extreme smoothness with easy tuning and rock stable reliability. That was in the hands of a good archer, not him.

He liked the pinpoint accuracy, in particular, he also wanted a new release aid, the type that fitted around the wrist.

He had had a bad experience of the other sort. He had been taught first of all on a recurve bow where the release was completely manual using a leather hand protector so that when moving to a compound bow he had aimed and fired, on the compound bow a tee piece release aid was used, with a trigger to shoot. He had released in the same way as he had on his recurve the release aid had stayed on the string and nearly took his fingers off. So there and then he had decided to stay with the wrist type, which prevented this from happening. To this end, he had brought his old release aid with him.

The reason he had changed from recurve was that he was worse than useless at it, and spent more time looking for lost arrows than shooting.

The experienced compound archer came to the door and invited him to where there was a display of different makers and specifications, and asked him what price range, make and style he wanted. He told him that he was interested in the XT 2000, but needed to make certain that it was good for him.

The advisor agreed that this was about the best bow, and also it was able to be paired up with a good range of extras.

"I have one set up, what weight do you want?"

Mike said, "40 pounds" – it would probably be as much as his arm could take.

"It is currently set at 30 pounds would you like to try it at that."

"Yes, that would be good."

He nocked the arrow and aimed at the centre of a target 40 metres away, he missed, the arrow was low, so the advisor altered the sight, he shot again, this time he hit the Boss or target, but still well down, with small adjustments, he got to near the bullseye and fired three arrows at it; the spread around the bullseye was within a handspan, and he knew that the way the bow was shaking in his hands that this was the best he could do without practice.

"Okay," he said, "this is the bow for me, what about sights release aids shall we sought that out now as well."

"No, the best time we can get this bow in is two weeks, so when it arrives make an appointment. We can sort out the rest of the attachments then. We will have them in stock and be able to tune everything to you then."

He paid for the bow and bought an elastic arm strengthener it was designed to get his muscles stronger and make pulling back the bow easier. It worked by using it exactly as if it was a bow, and by holding it in a prolonged ready to fire position, strain was put on the arm, strengthening it.

He would make an appointment for Jack, if home, to get his bow tuned at the same time, so they could work together. The bow had been light and only weighed about 2kg so that was good.

Once home, he rang up the secretary of the club that he used to belong to. He enrolled himself and Jack back into the club. The facilities there were second to none. They had the facility to shoot inside to 25 metres and it was open 24 hours a day as members had their own keys, and a combination code for the lock so he could use the facilities any time he chose. That included the kitchen with fridge, microwave, gas stove and tea making facilities. Outside, there was a safe range of 100 metres which had a raised earth bank behind to stop any rogue arrows from finishing in the field behind or hitting anyone. They would be pleased to see Mike and Jack again and they could start using the facilities immediately.

As the facilities were open day or night to him, he could pick and choose when he went.

They could also enter some field shoots, these consisted of targets placed at differing heights and terrain and distances from 20 to 100 yards. They would go when there were no lengths marked so they would have to guess the distance. They had seen bowmen on these ranges and there was always talk regarding estimating distances, some were uncannily accurate. The better estimate of distance allowed better accuracy.

There was a range within 10 miles of them at Kingsclere so it could be that joining this archery club could also be beneficial. It was in a good hilly valley.

Jack arrived home.

It was a shock when Mike heard the front door open, he had been deep in thought. He jumped up and went into the hall to find Jack struggling with a backpack and case on wheels. Mike rushed to him and covered him in a bear hug.

"Hell, I'm glad to see you, but what's happening, you are supposed to be at Uni for ages yet."

"I've taken my exams, and s'pose I could hang around at Uni, but think it would be better for all of us if I came home to help. Let me put my gear in my room, then we can have a cup of tea and you can tell me what's happened in detail and what's going to happen."

Jack rushed upstairs and slung his backpack on the bed and quickly unpacked his case, slinging dirty washing in the basket and clean stuff away in wardrobes and chest of drawers.

This done, he went back downstairs and sat down opposite Mike and sipped his tea.

Mike explained in detail what had happened, and the situation so far.

He explained to Jack that he wanted to be ready should he need to take a more pro-active approach, a rescue. Jack wanted to help, and as he said to his dad.

"Things are not looking good for Deb, so we really need to be absolutely ready with all options open, the way it's looking now we will need to do something ourselves. What is it they say?

"Hope for the best, but plan for the worst!"

Mike had already made up his mind that he was not prepared to risk Jack's life or liberty, so it would be down to him mainly but with Jack's invaluable help.

Jack went up finished unpacking, made up his bed, and took his washing down and put it in the washing machine.

Mike had gone into the garage and was busy checking over Jacks bike, his was in pretty good condition as he had used his up until he had left for this exam term.

Mike finished and he and Jack sat down and started to plan. Mike of course had already started, but he sorely needed Jack there to bounce ideas off.

Veronica came home and on seeing Jack ran over and gave him an almighty hug, "Oh God Jack it's good to have you home, maybe add some sanity to the situation."

~~~o~~~

The only way the prisoners knew that it was day was from a small barred opening in one of the walls. It was very small

63

so it never got beyond half-light here. The cell was only for one, and the bed as such was a narrow concrete ledge with a thin waterproof mattress and a thin blanket. There was a small pit which acted as a latrine in one corner, basically a hole in the floor which eventually drained away. Meals were once a day and not much of it. Water was given twice a day none for washing just for drinking. There was plenty of insect life, but no rodents thankfully. At first, she was tearful all the time, broken-hearted. It had taken a few weeks to realise that sitting there despondent was getting her nowhere so she had to think positively or at least a little bit positive. So she thought maybe meditation or yoga might help but they were things that she didn't do normally and had not done before so she would have to work out how to do it her own way.

The days and weeks seemed endless but she knew that her family would be doing all they could to get her home. There was also the court case, she hadn't been found guilty yet. She tried to merge the days so that she couldn't work out how long she had been there but she couldn't do it. Meditation did help a bit.

The days carried on and on and…

~~~o~~~

The main problem, if they weren't all big ones, was going to be the rescue itself to this end. They needed to know where to carry out the rescue. They knew where she was being held, and the building looked pretty fearsome, so that meant that she would only be able to be rescued when she was out of the prison, at Court, or on the way to or from it.

"We don't want to injure anyone, we don't want to escalate the rescue into something else," said Mike.

"I don't think that we should think about anything else until we've sorted out how to get out of the country."

"I've been thinking about transport, could we not hire a small plane and pilot? If there's a small airport, we could drive there, and fly out of the country."

Jack opened his laptop and brought up a map site, and zoomed in.

"There is an airport about 100 miles away, we could make for that."

"Yeah, but that's the only airport within miles, and probably has military or police helicopters stationed there."

"Okay, we need to put more thought into it. Let's look at that again later."

Mike grinned, "Let's re-cap on what we have so far, so what have we got:

"Need to be informed of when prison van leaves court.

"Need to be ready at ambush site and deploy stinger on hearing approach.

"When they get out of the car to repair the tyre, I need to threaten them with a bow with laser sight.

"Get Deb out of transport and get the hell out but not sure how yet."

Sure they had a lot to work out, but it was a start.

"We need to get out of the country, there are no airports nearby, and no direct access to the sea so the getaway can only be done by helicopter, road or walking. It's really got to be by road. Walking is out, it is their country, we know nothing about it, they were born there. They would have access to helicopters and dogs, we would soon be spotted and we don't know what condition Deb is in, she might not be up to a long hike. I haven't got a helicopter in my pocket and I would think that training to pilot one of those is far from easy, and there's no way I could afford to hire a pilot to do this."

"We need to think more about this, as you say it's got to be by road there must be a way."

"What about where to rescue her, I assume that the prison itself is out."

"Yes, there would be too many problems getting in and out of there and there would be too many guards around, and they would be armed. We will be told when Deb is due in court so that we can be there for her."

"We can work out from that what time she will be on her way, and if one of us is there we will know when she is going back."

"Right, so how are we going to get her out?"

"Well, we are going to have to get her out on the journey back, as if hopefully they say that she can or has to leave the country then we will obviously do nothing, but if it doesn't go that way then we need to act immediately."

"Yes, the court will be packed as I understand it."

"Yes! So it has to be on the journey back and in the evening to give us a chance to both get her and get out."

"Mmmm! Yes so, first of all, we have to stop the car or whatever she is being transferred by."

"We need to assume that she will be transferred by a van carrying at least three guards so to start off we need to stop it, then disable the guards."

"To stop a truck or car we need to either ram it or use a stinger. or we could use a roadblock, Road Closed? But I'm not sure they will take any notice of that."

"Yes! too obvious, and I expect they will guess something's not right as soon as they see it and they will have a radio in the transporter I would think."

They paused to think and get some more ideas.

"We need to stop the engine, if only we could shoot the bloody engine silently then they might believe the engine had just blown up and give us a chance of getting to them."

"Arrow!" said Mike, "we can shoot the engine with a bow and arrow but would it damage the engine enough to stop it."

"It would if you hit the engine front on through the radiator. As long as the engine is front on, or you go for a tyre, that might be better, they can't carry on with a flat, and you could possibly take out a second."

"They would see something and it's got to be simple and hopefully fool-proof, so it's got to be a stinger disguised so that they don't see it till they've gone over it. It's got to be on a bend."

"Yes! That's got to be the way, now what about the guards. If they have two flat tyres, it could be all of the guards get out. We need to quickly and silently disable the guards, preferably without injury."

"Let's come back to that, that's a big problem cause we have to stop them using the radio. Maybe we could jam the signal?"

"Let's start from where we ambush the van. One of us, you, need to be at the court, and let me know when they are leaving so that I can be ready. The road from the prison that she is being held at is pretty straight with few bends, we need to ambush the prison van when it slows down, which means that it has to be where there is a bend in the road, there are only a couple of places, and this bend here," Mike pointed to the map, "seems to be the best place, but it is only a couple of miles from the prison, which is on a hill, so not sure if the bend is completely visible to the prison guards."

"Well, on the plus side, they will be nearly home, so be a bit complacent hopefully."

"Yes, so let's assume that I have a stinger, I put it out and disguise it with leaves or something, the car stops, safely I hope and then I have to tackle two maybe three guards. How can I do that?"

"Some sort of drug attached to a syringe on an arrow?"
"Gonna have to work bloody quickly,"

"And accurate, best let me be the shooter."

"No, I'm not going to attempt to rescue one child at the expense of another, and possibly end with both of you in prison, I'd never be able to live with myself. How can we get some sort of anaesthetic? A hospital?"

"That would be easier said than done."

"Could the guards be coerced into surrendering with a bow and arrow aimed at them?"

"I could rig up a laser that would put a laser dot on them, if they run for the prison then I will aim for their legs to stop them unless I can get Deb into our car and away but need the keys if she is handcuffed."

"Your aim will need to improve."

"Yes, I know."

"Right, how are we to get away, there are no turn offs on this road for miles, I can't see how we can get away with it unless there is no hue and cry for several hours, and I drive like an F1 driver."

"Well, as we need to use a car, I don't know how much time we've got, they are going to know the roads much better than us, and as soon as its light, they will probably use a helicopter."

"Which means that we must be somewhere they are not expecting us to be, and be undercover by daylight."

"Yes, that's not going to be easy, and we've got to get out of the country, to a country which has no pact with them about the return of criminals, which is what we'll be."

~~~o~~~

"How's your bow, mine needs some use, so let's go and get a bit of shooting practice, take our minds off of it for a while."

"We aren't members anymore," said Jack.

"Yes, we are, I've sorted that," grinned Mike.

They went and got their equipment together, climbed into the car and Mike drove off.

About 15 minutes later, they turned off of the M3 onto the A303. They had travelled a mile or two down the road when a small plane roared overhead.

"He's coming into land at Popham," said Jack.

Mike didn't answer straight away.

"I've just thought of something," he said.

After passing the airport, he took the next turn off and followed it around under the A303 and to the back of the airdrome and through the entrance. There were several small aircraft parked there and six microlights in a line outside of a clubhouse.

Mike and Jack watched a couple of microlights in flight, taking off and landing. They looked at each other and grinned.

"Yes! We may have our way out."

"We need to start training," said Jack.

They decided to talk about it when they got home and carried on to the Archery Club.

They drove into the car park, Mike used the keypad and entered the code to open the door, it was already unlocked as other members were using it.

They went in and said hello to other archers, and as in the past, they knew that preparation was everything made a cup of tea.

They set their bows up ready, and went outside to the range, there was no-one else out there and so they had a choice of target.

"Let's go for 30 metres," said Jack.

The targets were on a trolley so that they could be moved to any distance then pegged down using ropes to hold them in the wind. Gone were the days of shooting at straw targets, now they used layered rubber and just pinned targets to it.

That set up their sights, aimed and fired, then altered the sights to get better accuracy. They shot for about an hour and a half, then packed up and drove home.

Mike bought a magazine on outdoor pursuits and flying. In it, he found numbers for several flying schools including the one at Popham, but rather than waste time phoning he decided to visit the airfield.

He drove down the M3 motorway and onto the A303 taking the turnoff for the airport. It was just before 3:00 when he arrived at the headquarters of the club.

He introduced himself explaining that he was interested in learning to fly a microlight and asked how and when he could learn, how long it would take and the cost.

Ron introduced himself, "I am the main instructor and I also run the Club."

The costs were quite prohibitive with the learning period which included various classroom exercises, and navigation as well as actually flying.

"I know it sounds expensive," said Ron, "I can see from your face that that was more than you wanted to pay, but there is another possibility.

"What we can do is first, you can become a member of the club, that will decrease the costs by 20%. Then if you buy a second-hand craft from us then it would be up to 50% off, the planes are no more expensive than any other place, and we service them and check them over well. You get to fly and try it.

"What sort are you after, one or two seats?"

"Two," Mike said.

"Okay that would mean one behind the other. Tandem, the passenger would sit slightly higher than the pilot. Let me show you a couple that we have at the moment. They both come with a trailer, tool kit and spares."

Ron said that he could peruse them at his leisure. He had a look at them and was taken by a Pegasus Q462 at a cost of £5350.

This also had the advantage of having a plain dark green canopy which could be ideal for camouflage. He would also get the discount on lessons as he wished to purchase a craft through them.

Ron asked Mike whether he would like to go up on a trial flight in a tandem plane then and there. He agreed to go with a little trepidation. He was supplied some overalls helmet and goggles and connected him to an intercom so they could talk.

They got themselves comfortable in the plane and Ron taxied it out onto the runway. He revved the craft up and away they went it seemed to travel no distance at all till it was airborne and he had that lurching feeling in his stomach as the plane soared rapidly higher and levelled off.

"Are you Okay?" Ron asked, "How do you like it?"

"Great," replied Mike.

He realised with a jolt that he really did, it was amazing.

Ron flew him around for a while and let him have a go with the controls giving him advice and praise as he became more confident. It seemed that they had only been up for a few minutes when Ron took control again and took them into land. He was enthralled to see how that would go but was well pleased with the way it met the ground with barely a bump.

They unstrapped and walked back to the office together. After removing their flying gear Mike said to Ron, "That was really great and I really enjoyed it, can't wait to go up again. When can I start taking lessons properly?"

"Just as soon as we sort everything out."

He gave the Pegasus a good look over and sat in it, he found it fairly comfortable and having examined it all over decided he would have it.

"Right, let's sort you out with a logbook. I know that you can take an intensive course down Amesbury way, but we don't do one here, the fact is that a short course is all well and good but it rushes things, you miss out on digesting each lesson, navigation can be a little heavy but it is essential. To get a full licence here takes about three months usually, but it is up to you exactly how long. What we do is book you in for lessons, and if the weather is against us we do one of the classroom ones."

Mike could see the sense of that and booked a course of lessons starting that week, he would try to have three lessons a week until he was allowed up on his own.

He even paid them a deposit insisting that after initial lessons in the club plane he would take his lessons in his one.

The Pegasus was easily stowed away for transport, had a joystick type control and a three-wheel undercarriage. It was also comfortable enough for him to fly size-wise and the passenger was located behind and slightly above him.

He left the aerodrome in a state of euphoria having recognised that he had made significant progress in fulfilling his goal. The rescue of Deb from jail.

"I've bought a plane," he told Jack.

"Didn't think you'd waste any time," he retorted.

Next day he went back, he needed to be able to fly as soon as he could.

"Hi Ron, been thinking, yes I need to get the navigation sorted out and other things as well, but I need to get a licence as soon as I can. Supposing I did the intensive course at Amesbury but still did some of the training lectures here as well?"

"Well, I know the head instructor over there, let me ring him and see how much it will cost and when he can fit you in."

He went to the phone and dialled the number, after a short chat, he called over to Mike, "Can you make next week?"

"Yes."

"Okay, you are booked in," he put down the phone. "When you get there ask for Jim Caraway, you need to take your plane with you."

"Okay."

"When you've earned your licence, we'll sort you out for some extra lessons."

"Have you got a towing hook on your car?"

"Yes, been using a trailer for years."

"Great, then you can take her away now."

"Be glad to, she will fit in my garage easily."

He backed in and hooked the microlight up, he gave Ron a wave and drove away.

It didn't take him long to get home, where he parked up outside the house, brought the small jockey-wheel at the front of the trailer down, and unhooked it then pulled it into his garage and shut the door.

He took the detailed drawings and assembly instructions of the plane that came with the manual and receipt indoors.

Jack sneaked a look at the receipt and took down the phone number. Then rang up.

"Hi, is that Ron?"

"Yeah, who is it?"

He asked Ron if as his father was taking the intensive course whether it would be possible for him to have the lessons that Mike was going to have cheap.

Ron laughed, "I suppose that you don't want him to know."

"Exactly," Jack replied.

"Yes okay. We can go up on Monday, whilst Mike is at his course, but you'll have to take out membership."

The following morning early Mike woke Jack for a morning ride. Although Mike had already started his training to get fit, Jack was way ahead of him.

Both Mike and Jack were ready to start training. They used the route Mike used and decided to cycle this in the mornings before the traffic got too busy. They could practice archery whenever and as often as they could, and would finish with a jog also on a set course of about three miles and increasing distance as soon as they felt they could, or rather when Mike felt he could, Jack could run that in his sleep.

They both realised that they needed to set themselves a regular exercise regime and keep it up, wind or shine.

They were out with their bikes at 6:30 a.m. Jack didn't find it too bad and made Mike increase his speed, so Mike had to stop a few times and get his breath. Thoughts of his daughter kept him going though. They followed the same exercise route that he had found.

Mike had worked it out that they would cycle this route until they could both finish it without being too short of breath, this clockwise route although being hilly was nothing like cycling the anticlockwise route, the hills were steeper in this direction. On the whole, it was an enjoyable route with plenty to see. Mike found that using his iPod with only one earphone was good and allowed him to hear what was happening around him as well as hearing his favourite music.

Whoever finished first was first in the shower. Mike never got near and always sat down with a cup of tea waiting impatiently for Jack to finish. Mike would then give Jack a lift to his part-time job as a process worker in a nearby factory, he would then carry his other plans forward.

The first few weeks flew by, Mike and Jack were getting fitter, and the cycle route was getting quicker and quicker. Neither of them had to stop now. That is except for the day when Mike had managed to get a puncture and had to walk home. Fortunately, he was three-quarters of the way around, so it wasn't too far. Mike decided that it was time to reverse the route. The same sights were getting a bit boring, and at least going the opposite direction should stop them getting dizzy.

~~~o~~~

Now that he had the plane home Mike could attach extras which were needed and to this aim, he had a list.

Bow with all accessories fitted, this was red laser light and Telescopic sight.

Sleeping bag, coat; Veronica was even now modifying sleeping bags so that they were also coats and fitted to the seats, this way they could wear them when flying and to sleep in.

Tarpaulin camouflaged for the jungle one side and the desert on the other.

Water containers

Stinger, he needed to get one of these

Food dried

Stove to heat water

Spare clothing for Deb

Binoculars

Radio: all-purpose transmit and receiver

Lights for landing, as he intended to fly at night.

Rear lights, it occurred to him that if the guards saw rear red lights on the back disappearing up the road, they would think that he was in a car.

The aim is to make or buy fittings to house the items, whilst keeping weight to a minimum. The plane had its own tool kit, which was a bonus.

He looked on the internet to see whether there was anything that he could buy for storage, they must make something.

He found that the makers of the microlight made several extras:

A tarpaulin which was light and coloured in jungle type camouflage colour one side, and dessert type colouration on the reverse.

A storage locker that fitted beneath the rear passenger's seat, as the passenger was at the back of the craft, and raised slightly above the pilot, there was room to fit the locker between the engine and passenger, it wouldn't take much inside, but he could fit the camouflage canopy in it as well as other spares such as patching for the wings, glue etc.

He bought some lights for landing at night and rear lights normally used on a bicycle.

~~~o~~~

In the evenings, after they had finished training, Veronica, Jack and he would sit down and try to plan things out.

It came to him that he had to get the craft across to a neighbouring country to where he wanted to get too, but be in range of the prison.

They made another list.

Transport for the microlight to a nearby country

Get information on the prison, courthouse and transport

microlight training course

Sort out his bow (Mike's)

Finish sorting out their escape route

Refuelling, they wouldn't get out on a mere tank full of petrol.

He assembled everything in his garage, alongside of the plane minus wings of course, but assembled away from the trailer sitting proudly on its own undercarriage.

He made clips so that the bow could be easily extracted and be able to shoot. And also that the stinger was clipped in as well.

He put everything then into where it was going to be stored when the plane took off. It was all secure and wouldn't fall off, but it would need to be checked in flight.

He had checked the weight and it was fine so hopefully, everything was good and ready, the bow would come free easily as well. Arrows were held close by.

He would take it all to the airfield when he had finished his training and give it all a go, sort of dry run, with Jack on board to make certain that it would be okay with Deb on board.

Finalising the plan had to be sorted so they knew exactly what they had to do, so to this end, the three of them Veronica, Jack and Mike sat around the dinner table with a coffee each.

Veronica started first, "There is no way that Jack is entering Berithroa," she looked at him, "there will surely be things to do here away from the action."

Mike agreed.

"Let me outline my plans again, I will fly in the day before the trial and get prepared, I do not intend to hurt anyone, but I will if I have to but not to the point of causing death.

"So although I will have my bow with me I will not use it unless I have to.

"However, I need to get landing areas ready beforehand with petrol cans installed as well as oil etc for the plane, so to this end, I intend to fly into a neighbouring country and recruit some local help.

"I also need to look at getting out through other countries and they are friendly with Berithroa so that too has to be done quietly."

"Let me do that," said Jack. "I have a few ideas I can fly to Algiers, hire a 4x4 and sort out the landing strips. I can order the equipment and have it shipped to a local warehouse where I can collect it.

"Also while we are about it, how do you intend to land in the dark? I know you have landing lights and GPS but looking at instruments and trying to land is a recipe for disaster. So to that end, I want to put in landing lights, the lights can be the type shaped like rocks and are turned on by a transponder which turns the lights on from a switch in the cockpit and work from a mile away."

"That sounds great," said Mike.

"Also, we need to get across to Europe and safely, and are looking to fly across the sea near Gibraltar. Leave that to me to sort out.

"How does a charity flight appeal to you? We have two microlights remember, we could be flying a charitable mission to get funds for a local hospice, I reckon I can cover for you on the way there, as it is only flight plans they will be interested in. I will join you from when you leave Algiers and we fly home to Popham together with our photographer, Deb."

"Sounds a bit unethical to me," said Mike.

"At first, look, yes but we are taking nothing from them, and I will sort out an online donation site which pays the charity directly, so we have no contact with the money, and European authorities will want to help us. So we both gain."

After a few minutes of thought, Veronica said, "As Jack said we both win, however little we raise it all goes to the charity, and we get the cover."

"Okay," said Mike. "Go for it, and on that point, we are ready to go.

"Veronica will be in the court to let us know whether to go ahead with the rescue and if we do then she needs to get out of the country as soon as possible."

~~~o~~~

Getting off the plane was like walking into a wall, the humidity and heat taking his breath away. He walked along with the other passengers to what looked like a large brick built shed. As he queued to enter it, he noticed the inoculation room on his right, it looked extremely unsanitary – he congratulated himself on having his at home in England.

Collecting his luggage was the next step, from the steel rotating conveyor which was pre-war. He elbowed his way out to the front and through an open hatch he could see the workers unloading the baggage from the aircraft on an old trailer drawn by a tractor with no tyres. The handlers then threw the cases through a hatch onto the conveyor. He hoped that his case could take the abuse.

Passengers started moving away having already rescued their bags, and eventually, there was but a handful of people left. Panic began setting in, the sweat dripping from his forehead and into his eyes, not all of it from the heat. At last, he saw his suitcase appear and with a sigh of relief grabbed it and made his way to customs. He was handed a form to fill out saying how much money he was bringing into the country.

As he approached the customs desks, he saw in alarm one of the officers gesture to a German passenger from another flight to put his suitcase onto the table. He rummaged through his case, then pushed it off the end, clothes and bits and pieces going everywhere. The German picked it all up and into his case muttering something that could only be detrimental to the officer, if he had understood it. Then it was his turn but after organizing his money form was gestured through.

On walking through the next doors, he found himself outside the airport. Before he had time to draw a breath he was accosted by half a dozen taxi drivers.

"Where are you going?" they asked him. He tried to explain that he was waiting for his courier from the travel company. A young white woman came to his aid and spoke in their language. She smiled and introduced herself as the courier, and was he Mr Thornton, as the coach was waiting for him.

A young man grabbed his case and walked with them to a dilapidated coach and the driver loaded his case onto it whilst he made himself comfortable inside. The girl introduced herself to the tourists and also another man who was the main courier for the hotel where he was staying, and whilst they talked about the various excursions etc Mike took a big breath of relief. He was in Africa at last.

The relief was a little premature as all the drivers felt that they were racing drivers and the roads never mind the drivers were not up to speed of any kind, the coach lurching around corners and bouncing across the large holes in the tarmac. He complained about the roads in Britain but these roads did not compare.

He soon learnt to keep his head down or risk serious concussion when he was thrown from his seat and his head made contact with the luggage rack above every few minutes. The main safety apparatus on board wasn't the brake, but the horn, as the driver seemed under the illusion that as he was ferrying Europeans around he had right of way over everyone else.

Although he had seen a video of the city, he was surprised at the amount of smiling happy faces that he saw considering the living conditions, and yet, when considering the destitute people in his own capital, it wasn't that far removed, a bed in a brick room, compared to a corrugated one here. And the weather here was warmer. Everywhere he looked there were shops selling beds and furniture, all looked to be made from hardwood and well crafted.

The coach arrived at a ferry across a large river and stopped. The courier explained that they would have to leave the coach and go as foot passengers until they reached the other side, the reason being that a lorry had managed to drive off the end of the ferry recently. The courier would stay on the coach to protect their belongings, so all baggage could remain on board.

The tourists joined the locals in queueing to get on the boat, it was like a game of sardines, and the smell of stale sweat hung over the boat like a blanket. The ferry itself was just a larger version of the Isle of Wight Ferry, and after about 19 minutes they were all safely across.

They walked up a hill and waited in the comparative shade of a large tree with kids trying to sell them cashew nuts and papers until at last the coach emerged and they were able to climb back on.

The coach drove past small villages where all the houses had plots of land with fruit growing in them – bananas, pineapples etc. In the countryside, there were many exotic plants growing, the landscape was beautiful.

The coach slowed down and swerved from one side of the road to the other, there was a bang and the coach screeched to a halt. Three policemen and four soldiers ran to the door on the bus. He noted the automatic rifles the soldiers carried. Looking out of the rear of the coach, Mike could see that they had passed through a police checkpoint, the swerving was because laid in the road was a set of 4" spikes across one side of the road, and another set further back on the other side, causing a sort of chicane. The coach had caught one of its rear tyres on the edge of one of these and it had ripped to shreds.

There was a long and heated debate involving the policemen, the courier and the driver, whilst the soldiers watched on nonchalantly with shouldered weapons. Eventually, the driver got back behind the wheel and they carried on with their journey. The courier explained that the driver was going to be charged with careless driving, the coach would stop at the first hotel, and they would continue their travels by taxi, as it was dangerous with only one out of the double wheeled tyres serviceable.

They arrived at the first hotel which unfortunately wasn't Mike's, and everyone had to get off. Mike was ushered into an ancient Mercedes. The windscreen was badly cracked, the doors didn't close properly and he could see the road through the floor. This probably accounted for the fact that the seat wasn't even bolted down. He and two others were catapulted down the road by the grinning taxi driver until 10 minutes later they arrived at their hotel.

They passed the security hut where the guard opened the gates to allow them access. They went down a long drive with bougainvillaea blossom hedging the way to the reception. They got out of the taxi and were greeted by smiling porters who took their cases inside and gave them ice-cold tropical fruit cocktails which were both delicious and refreshing. After sitting down to get their breath back, the porters were ready to take them to their rooms. Mike was taken back out into the grounds where there were many round thatched buildings all painted white.

Mikes room was on the top floor, one of the top rooms. Each building consisted of four rooms, two top and two bottom. On entering, he was astounded at how cool it was, thanks to the air conditioning. The room was clean and comfortable, and after tipping the porter he closed the door and surveyed the room properly.

There was plenty of space with wardrobes and draws and even the bed, being obviously hand-finished and fitted, no cheap chipboard here and built by craftsmen. He sat on the bed and was impressed at the comfort; the bathroom was also spacious with a choice of bath or shower. Adjoining the room was a set of patio doors leading on to a balcony with chairs and tables. He could see monkeys in the palm trees opposite. He rang reception and asked for an alarm call in one and a half hours' time, the bed was beckoning him and he undressed and lay on it and fell asleep.

It seemed only a minute or so since he had closed his eyes when the phone woke him, but if he had slept any longer he would have been jet-lagged. It was tempting to lay there for a little longer, but he forced himself to get up, shower and unpack his bags.

After hanging his clothes up, he dressed in shorts and t-shirt and wandered down to reception. The bar was open so he bought himself a beer which was ice cold. He wandered over to the notice boards and read with interest the sports itinerary available from morning runs to water polo. He decided to go for an exploring walk.

He walked down to the shore, where street traders were waiting to sell their wares to any tourists that wished to buy. There were security guards also whose job was to keep the traders moving, they could only stop if invited by one of the hotel guests.

About 50 yards from the shore was a reef, this side of it was a sandbank and the water was quite shallow, but not walkable. The reef on the other side dropped down sharply and was very deep. He could see people walking along the sandbank.

The beach people were selling rides out to the reef on the outrigged boats with sails. The price as with all things here had to be negotiated and Mike loved to haggle as it appeared so did the locals.

One of the people doing the ferrying and haggling stood out to Mike and caught his eye, he must have stood out to this beach seller as well as he made a beeline for him.

They negotiated for a trip across to the reef and back, a price was agreed and Mike got into the boat, the seller told him his name was Ben, and the other guy in the boat was Donald. They all shook hands and Ben explained that Mike was now his client and whenever he wanted to go out to the reef and back, he was the man to take him.

On his part, he liked the partnership of Ben and Donald, they were all smiles especially when Donald nearly fell in when trying to get the sail up. They chatted and Ben intimated that if Mike wanted anything, he was the person to get it for him in.

Mike had a walk along the sandbank and watched the other hotel guests, but mainly the beach sellers, it could be that he had made a valuable contact, but he would wait, watch and see. A bit later he waved to Donald, and he and Ben collected him. He thanked them and walked back to the hotel.

Mike collected a towel and stretched out on a sunbed, one of the staff scaled up a coconut palm tree, making it look easy. He cut down coconuts with a machete and let them drop to the sand beneath. He came down and using the sharp machete, he chipped the top of the fruit and offered it to all the guest with a straw. The milk was cool and sweet and a cold drink, he found it refreshing especially as he was melting. The sun loungers were placed on a grass patio.

The grass was a small area, and it was not turfed but planted individually, he saw a gardener digging some in. In the centre of the area, there was a large bushy tree which had many black splats around it and there was a flock of hornbills in the tree scoffing blackberries and made a mental note to keep away from it he didn't want his shirt dyed.

It was a great position to watch the beach traders. In a far corner of the beach, he could see an Asian man, he was organizing the sellers, supplying the merchandise, the cost and directing them to tourists as they appeared. He was the orchestrater.

Ben and Donald, had no contact with him, he noticed that they had the respect of the guards as well as the other beach traders.

Also during the time he was watching, if the tourist games were short of a place or two, then they would make up those places.

He carried on watching to the end of the day, then went back to his room, changed and went to dinner. This was followed by a few drinks, then bed.

Breakfast was good the next morning, Weetabix then fruit. He had found his bed comfortable and slept quite soundly.

At a reasonable time, a little past 10 a.m., he changed into his swimming gear, then carrying his snorkel gear and wandered down to the beach. Donald was swimming and came out of the sea shivering.

"How long have you been in there?"

"Ten minutes."

"You are shivering, are you okay, not ill or something?"

"No! it's just so cold."

"Blimey, it's so warm I could stay in there till I shrivel up."

He got into the boat and watched as they put up the sail.

Ben said that they had once worked in a hotel bar, and had gone into a refrigerated room where they kept food, just to see what it was like.

"Couldn't live in a country like yours that was too cold, no way."

Mike laughed.

They reached the reef and he got off and went into the water with his mask and snorkel. He watched the colourful fish and swam thinking about how he was going to approach Ben and Donald with his plan.

He decided to come straight out with it well what he wanted them to help him with anyway. He carried on swimming around for about an hour and a half, then went to the edge of the reef sand and waved to Ben and Donald. They brought the little boat back and he got in.

"Enjoy that," said Ben.

"Yeah, that was good," he waited till they were a little distance away from the reef and other tourists who were using the reef.

"Do me a favour, take in the sail. I have a little proposition for you."

They looked at each other a bit intrigued, but did as he asked. Sat down in the boat and waited for him to explain.

"I have to get into Berithroa and make three places where a land-rover can refuel, secretly, the trouble is that I don't speak the language. I need to get petrol and bury it so that it isn't found. I need good petrol cans, I need to put five gallons at each place, so 15 one-gallon cans.

"You two know this country and I'm sure you have contacts that can get the cans and know where to get the petrol from, there are a few other things I need to bury, water and food supplies. I can assure you that drugs are not involved. I need to know whether you are in for this or not. We'll talk about money if you can do what I ask and not tell anyone.

"Think about it and we'll talk about it tomorrow, let me assure you as I say drugs are not involved. I have watched you, and believe that you are well respected in the community, would that be right?"

"Yes, we work for ourselves, and gradually we are getting to a place that we have been working where our families are proud of us, but we are only just breaking even, and we have no wish to get back into a debt that we used to be in."

"Well, you know the country, and the risks, it is up to you whether to go or not, I don't want you to risk anything, but there obviously is an element of risk. Obviously, I do not want you to do this for nothing but there is a limit to what I am able to pay for you, so it is for you to tell me how much you want?"

"So what is the plan?"

"I can't tell you that until I know whether you are with me or not.".

They agreed to think about it overnight as he explained that he had to go early in the morning the day after next.

~~~o~~~

Jack left home at about 6:00 in the morning and walked to the railway station, it took him about 30 minutes with his case and flight bag, the case had wheels and an extendable handle, which made it easy for him to walk with, he had to collect his tickets from a ticket machine; he had already ordered them online.

He went to the platform, where the train to Clapham Junction would stop, it arrived pretty much on time. He got on and was a little surprised to find that most of the seats had been already taken, but managed to get his case on a luggage rack and sat down beneath it. The train was a fast one and didn't stop at many stations.

The train pulled into Clapham and he got off and caught his connection to Gatwick, it was also fast and only stopped at East Croydon, then Gatwick.

Checking that he was at the correct terminal, and queued up to check-in and got rid of his case. The girl who was serving at the check-in desk asked him for his passport and boarding pass. He placed his case on the weighing conveyor belt, the weight was okay, she placed a tag through the handle and it disappeared, she handed him back his passport and he went to the duty-free gate.

He took off his belt and placed his bag in a tray and onto the conveyor there and put his wallet mobile phone and change into another. He went through the metal detector, and his passport and boarding pass were checked again and he was nodded through to collect his stuff and carry on into duty free.

A coffee was what he desperately needed, and so his next visit was to a coffee bar where he bought a large latte to take away and found a place to sit and wait for the gate for his flight to open. He had got himself a seat where he could see the flight display screen.

It said on the screen, that his gate would open in about one and a half hours' time. He took out a paperback from his bag and sat down to read it. After his second cup of coffee, the sign changed and he had to go to gate 10 for embarkation.

He tried to remain calm, but even though the journey had been straightforward he was still jittery. He followed the directions to gate 10 and took a seat in the waiting area there and waited for the staff at the security desk to start the boarding process.

They called the passengers up by seat number blocks, filling the plane from the centre outwards using the front and back doors. His turn came and he had to show his passport and boarding card again and passed down the long corridor and then umbilical cord that connected the plane doors to the airport.

He showed the stewardess there his boarding pass and made his way to his seat. He put his hand luggage in the overhead storage locker first retrieving his book and headphones, then sat down in his seat which was nearest the window. There were three seats and he wondered who would be travelling with him.

A middle-aged couple put their flight bags into the lockers after taking out their requirements for the journey, they smiled a hello and sat down. The staff went through the emergency procedures and the plane's engines started. The plane turned and taxied to the runway and took its place in the queue for take-off.

He took out a hard-boiled sweet which he would suck till they had reached the full altitude as this would help with his ears popping. He offered them to the couple sitting next to him, but they waved their own bag.

"Thank you but we have some already."

The plane moved forward, and nearly stopped, then the engines wound up to take off speed and with a lurch as the brakes came off, they thundered down the runway and took off. It was to be a seven-and-a-half-hour flight so the sooner the better.

As soon as they were flying steadily, the stewards and stewardesses brought round coffee or tea, and an hour later, some food. After he had finished, he settled down and fell asleep, making up perhaps for what he hadn't had the night before. He awoke to find them bringing round drinks again and looking at the onboard monitors saw that they were past the halfway point. But he still had another three hours to fly so he settled back down, he looked through the window, but there was nothing to see except clouds.

He couldn't get back to sleep so he read his book for a while, the couple next to him seemed asleep. After about an hour, he felt a bit drowsy and went back to sleep, it was dark outside and he knew that with the difference in time zones it would be morning when they landed. His work would begin as soon as he landed.

~~~o~~~

Next morning, a hired land rover was delivered to Mike at the hotel in his name.

He took it down to the city docks to a warehouse that he had arranged for the equipment he had bought to be delivered. He had made sure that his phone was fully charged as it had an app on it for satellite navigation.

He drove to where a security barrier was across the road with a guard inside, he handed over his passport and documents showing that he had come to collect some crates that had been delivered and stored here.

The guard looked at the location and pointed him in the direction of the store. There was an office there so he went in and gave his paperwork to another official. He was shown where the boxes awaited him and given a pallet truck to take them out to the Land Rover.

He checked that for damage and that everything was there, then re-packed them so that he could pack them easily into the land rover. With room for the other containers.

All done, he drove out of the compound, he forgot himself in his eagerness to get away and started to drive on the left instead of the right, then seeing a lorry coming towards him, he quickly changed lanes and entered the bedlam of traffic in the city. With his heart in his mouth, and hand on the horn, he made his way out, and back to his hotel and parked up.

He changed into his snorkelling gear and went down to the beach, and signalled to Ben that he wanted to go out to the reef. Ben and Donald brought the boat back from the reef where they had just ferried customers out.

He got into the boat.

"Hi, have you made a decision? I need to go tomorrow early."

"Yes, we're in, depending on the money and exactly what we have to do."

"Okay, I'll drive us to the places I need to get to. I'm not telling you where exactly, but they are away from habitation. I need for you to get the containers and fuel for me, good quality stuff. We will be away for three days."

"Right, it's still risky so we would want $1500 between us, how does that sound?"

"I'm not going to argue with that, but I will give you $1500 when we get back, and I will pay you another $500 when I've completed the expedition in a couple of months. I will come back to the hotel and see you then."

He also gave them a further $300 for the petrol and any other expense they came across.

"Deal," they both agreed, an extra $500 would be good and they would trust him for that.

"4 a.m. tomorrow, outside the hotel gates, wave me down out of sight."

"Okay."

They reached the reef, he got out and went snorkelling. After an hour, he called them back and went back to the hotel.

"See you tomorrow at four," said Ben.

They laughed and with a shock, he saw that Ben and Donald were looking forward to it.

That's good he said to himself, they will play their part.

"Right," he said.

As soon as it got dark, he got changed and went to dinner in the restaurant then went into the bar had a couple of cold beers then went to his room, set his alarm and went to bed.

~~~o~~~

The plane circled once before it could land, Jack was sucking on his second sweet by now as he had started to feel the pressure difference on his ears earlier. Touch down was smooth and the plane taxied to its designated position and the engines turned off. They waited for what seemed like an age before the doors were opened. He waited patiently for a gap in the queue to get out of the door, then climbed out of his seat grabbed his flight bag and took his turn getting off the plane and onto a bus for ferrying the passengers to the terminal building.

He had put his paperback and headphones in his bag and followed the other passengers through passport control where they checked that he had also got certificates for the various inoculations he had needed. Then to collect his luggage, which he retrieved from the circular conveyor after waiting for some time for it to be ferried from the aircraft hold.

He walked through customs, where he was ushered straight through, probably because his case was so small, and it was obvious that he was not going to be there long, and didn't have much room in his case for contraband.

It was a sort of relief to get to the outer part of the terminal, but he had now to pick up the transport that he had organised. He looked at all the hire company stalls, which were numerous until he found the one that he had booked with. On presenting his passport, he was shown outside to a largish four by four, it was very very big. He slung his case in and started her up, she started easily and sounded good.

He showed the hire car man the address of where he had to get to, the guy gave him a map and drew on it where he had to go. Great, it was just around the corner and about two miles away. He had seen what the place looked like when he had hired space in the warehouse on his computer.

Driving across, he was pleased to see that the roads were not too busy. He drove to the security gate and showed his paperwork, he was ushered to a lorry entrance, where he showed a worker there his paperwork. The man disappeared and then reappeared with two pallets on a forklift truck, he put them down beside the offloading ramp and drove away.

Jack undid the strapping and put in the boxes of supplies. Then he unpacked the second pallet which was full of petrol cans. He removed them from their packaging and put them all in covering the other boxes so that he had two complete layers of cans. He then placed all the cardboard packaging on top of them and got into the driver's seat just as a lorry arrived to collect other stuff.

He drove out and using the sat nav on his phone, made his way towards the route that he and Mike had planned. He came to a petrol station and noticed that lorries went round the back to fill up, and did likewise.

He removed the top layer of petrol cans, and removed the lids from the second layer, then filled them up closing the lids as he filled them. He placed some of the cardboard packaging over them and the put the other layer in removing the lids as he went, then he filled these up and put the caps on and put the rest of the cardboard on them.

He checked that he had plenty of fuel in the 4x4, checked that he had two spare tyres and that the air pressure was okay in all of them, then went in to pay. He had a quick look around the sales floor and picked up some food and bits of pieces, he loaded up 20 large bottles of water then went to the till. He was surprised that they were using chip and pin payment devices, so inserted his card and put in the pin. The attendant handed him a receipt with a bored look as if he had seen it all before.

He walked back to his car. He drove out and along to the town of Oran. He turned on to the N6 and followed it for a few miles, before he got to the town of Mascara. He turned off about five miles from the road and parked up for the night. He took out a shovel and started digging, he dug a hole large enough to bury the petrol cans needed, ten of them. He placed some cardboard over them and buried them, then placed a spanner on top so that they could be found. Next after drinking some water himself, as it was so hot, he slung the hat which protected him from the sun and dug another hole, this time burying some water and food and a note.

~~~o~~~

The alarm went off on his phone, and although he felt that he had hardly slept, he had managed a few hours. He showered and dressed and was ready, he waited till it was 3:45 a.m. and went to the Land Rover, switched on the ignition and started the engine. He gave it a couple of minutes to settle down, then drove out of the hotel gates opened by a security guard. He drove slowly down the road and round a bend out of sight of the guardhouse. Ben and Donald were waiting down the road. He stopped and they got in.

"Right, we need to get the petrol cans and fill them up. Drive for a while and I will tell you when to turn off."

15 minutes later and Donald told him to turn right. He did so and came immediately to a garage.

There were petrol cans stacked ready to go.

"We filled them last night so we just need to put them in the wagon."

Mike quickly took out some of the boxes that he had packed the day before and they placed the petrol cans in the middle of the back luggage section, and some on a roof rack above. They covered everything with a tarpaulin and were ready to go in 30 minutes.

They set off, Mike using the Sat Nav he had brought with him.

"Be careful," Ben said, "there are many baboons around at this time and if you should hit one we must carry on, as, if you get out, others will attack you."

After a couple of hours, the sun was up and they were travelling faster.

"Pull in here," Donald said.

"We will get out and meet you down the road after the Border post. About a mile up the road is a clearing on the left, so stop and we will meet you there."

Ben and Donald jumped out and disappeared into the bush.

Mike drove to the check-point, showed his passport and was waved through with no checks at all.

He found the clearing and waited for Ben and Donald to appear. 10 minutes later, he saw them, and with a furtive look left and right to check for any activity, hopped back into the Land Rover. They both gave him a sardonic grin.

The first point of call was to scout out the ground around the prison, specifically where the ambush was to take place.

So he needed to get to the bend near the prison, but not be seen. He drove using the sat nav directions to where the bend in the road was. There was vegetation on either side of the road, which he took pictures of to look at camouflage when he got home. The road surface was pretty good, certainly okay to land and take off from, and it was about two miles from the prison itself. It was nearly dark when they arrived there, so he had to be fairly quick to find a place off of the road where they could stop safely overnight.

About 30 yards from the bend was a small gap in the undergrowth which he drove off on, it looked as if it had been made by a truck or tractor or something.

They all jumped off the land-rover.

"Right, let's get the area a bit smoothed out, but leave the front alone as it is, and try to make it so that it looks as if nothing has passed through it recently."

This they quickly did. Mike helped them dig a hole and placed the petrol cans in and the stinger parts in the hole, then filled it back up and spread leaves over it.

They got back into the car and Mike poured them some drinks and food that he had brought in a refrigerated hamper.

"We need to keep an eye out tonight, so we must take it in turns to stay awake."

They settled down for the night.

~~~o~~~

That night Jack slept in the car, he didn't sleep well again and kept hearing noises outside in the shadows of the starry but intense dark undergrowth. Even though he was wrapped up in his hooded sleeping bag, he still felt cold. In the morning, whilst it was getting lighter, he paced out the landing area installed the lights transponder and after checking the direction with a compass, he took out his Garmin and saved the co-ordinates, then removed as much evidence of his having been there as he could. He started the engine then drove back onto the N6. He drove through Mascara, where he didn't see many people other than goatherds bringing the goats in for feeding and milking. He carried on down the N6 and after five hours came to Tawrirt. There was a tee junction where the N6 met the N52, he carried on the N6 for another few miles then turned off onto a track, the road got bumpy and there were several times that he thought that he would get bogged down. The car was skittish and bouncing into hidden dips filled with sand. After about twenty miles, he stopped got out some binoculars and looked around, there was no-one about. He drove about 200 yards off of the track, walked around and tested the surface, it was sound and would do nicely.

He dug a hole for the petrol cans and put them into the hole, then he added a weatherproof bag and filled it in, covering the cans with cardboard, he placed a spanner on top of the smoothed down petrol dump.

He marked out the landing strip again using a compass for direction. He placed the landing lights and transponder into position. He heated up some water on his primus stove and made some tea, this refreshed him a bit, and he followed that up with some food not much, but enough to take the edge off of his hunger. He settled down in his transport for a second uncomfortable night's sleep. He was knackered so thought that he would sleep okay, but it was not to be.

~~~0~~~

As soon as day broke the next morning, they checked everything was covered and Mike drove back onto the road, whilst Donald kept an eye out. He and Ben used a few pieces of brushwood to sweep the tyre tracks away off of the road, jumped back in the car and Mike quickly drove down the road.

Luck was with them and they didn't meet any traffic at all. It wasn't very well used.

"Well, that's the first stop done," he smiled at Donald and Ben. They made a right turn and three hours later, Mike came to a track made years ago, it was a bit overgrown, but was just visible on Satellite maps. He turned off and they slowed down to a very bumpy 20 miles an hour. They drove following the track for about two hours then Mike stopped for them all to stretch their legs.

Another couple of hours and Mike turned slowly off of the track till he came to a small clearing; the ground was hard but a little bumpy in places.

They got out, stretched and took some spades, rake and fork out. He examined the ground and checked his compass, he quickly decided on the runway. The idea was to put in one row of lights 20 feet apart and then he would land to the left of them.

To one side he stuck in a spade.

"This is for the cans," he said to Donald and Ben. They unpacked six cans and began to dig a pit for them. Whilst they did that, he used a spade and rake to smooth out the landing area.

Ben and Donald finished digging their hole and put in the cans, then put cardboard over them and filled the hole in. They used the dried top soil to disguise that anything had been buried, and topped it off with three stone in a triangle close together as a marker. Mike had only to position the lights.

Whilst he did that, he gave Donald and Ben some bottles of water and they buried them as they had the petrol cans and a container of tinned food and a small gas burner. The container that the food was in was also made from aluminium and served as a saucepan.

Mike had put in the lights, they were disguised as rocks, ran on batteries and were connected to each other by wire, and at the end was the transponder which he could activate from about a mile away. He tried it out using a small handheld transmitter and it was working fine.

He covered the cables up and raked the area again. By this time Ben and Donald had finished putting in the water and supplies which also had a plastic tube with extra arrows with them.

"Another one down," he grinned, and they set off again, it would be dark in a few hours and he would like to get a bit nearer to the next landing site.

~~~o~~~

Following his disturbed night, it was a relief for Jack to see the dawn and sun come up. He quickly strolled around the site making certain that he had left nothing behind, then climbed back into the van having tied some old brushwood he had found on the trail behind to help obliterate his track. He drove back to the main road and after making certain that nothing was coming, got out and strapped the brushwood back on the top of the wagon, climbed back in and carried on down the tarmacked road.

After another two hours, the scenery began to change, the sand became much more compacted and solid, and he could see mountains in the distance. He was grateful that he had a tarmac road to follow and that he could get a fair speed up which at least gave him some relief from the heat. Another hour passed and he came to a crossroad, to left and right he saw that the road was no longer tarmac but just a dusty track. He turned on to it, bringing his speed down to 20mph.

He came close to the town of Achemelmel, there was an air-strip here and he wanted Mike to be able to steer clear of it. After a couple of hours, he was in the mountains, the road mainly followed the valleys in the mountains, but even so, it was very up and down and sometimes took his breath away when he came round a bend and he found himself on a precipice with a lot of space between the track he was on and the bottom. His speed had gone right down and sometimes he was crawling along. Gradually, he became aware that it was flattening out a bit, and he was becoming a little used to the track and his speed was climbing so it was with relief that he found himself within five miles of Aguelhok and drove off the track for a couple of miles and stopped.

Here he would put his last landing strip. He had to take out a pickaxe as the ground was so hard, but not too bad, it crumbled as soon as his pickaxe hit it and he was soon down to a good depth, and put the petrol cans in with the cardboard over them and buried them, then he dug another hole and placed the spare parts in and closed that up. He then paced out the air-strip and put in the lights and transponder.

It was dark now and as Jack was close to a town and also only a couple of miles off the road, he dared not use any light, so it was water to drink and cold food. He had these in his sleeping bag, but had the luxury of being able to stretch out in the back of the motor as he now had nothing left there but his own water and fuel. He set his alarm as he wanted to be away as soon as it was light; he had a long way to go, and knew it would take a day or so.

~~~o~~~

Mike followed the road for a couple of hours then pulled off onto a track and reached the lake. Mike could see the island some way off. He brought the Land Rover to some brush with a bit of cover.

"Well, we have done pretty well to get here already, now you need to get a boat if you can, to get to the island, whilst it's dark would be good."

Donald and Ben set off to get a boat. They hadn't said how or where they were going to get it from; he didn't ask but just had to trust them.

He unloaded the equipment that they needed to get across and waited for them in the Land Rover. He heard the boat coming towards him and flashed his torch to show where he was and watched it beach. There was no time for chat now, they loaded the little boat out with the equipment and off they all went. It was very low in the water.

It didn't take too long to get to the island, they unloaded all the gear that they needed and carried everything over to a flat part the island. Mike marked where the petrol had to be hidden and another for where the other parts and water needed to be buried.

Whilst they buried the petrol and other parts, Mike went over to the landing site which was pretty good. He connected the wiring and laid it all out where he wanted the lights, then fitted the transponder and tested them briefly, they all worked so he buried the wiring and had a quick look round the island. On the maps, he had seen a small lake on it and he wanted to test it to see whether it was fresh spring water. He tasted it and yes, it was good.

They finished what they were doing put the tools back in the boat and Mike had a quick look around the island to make certain they had left nothing behind and everything was hidden. He got in the boat with them and they sailed across the lagoon and he got out where he had got on.

Whilst Donald and Ben took the boat back to wherever they got it from, Mike cooked food on the small primus stove he had brought with them. Ben and Donald came back just in time cause dinner was ready. He went into the back of the car and opened another lunchbox, it was connected to the electrics and was full of cold beer. He handed them each a couple. They sat and enjoyed the food and beer.

They went back into the car to sleep in it that night. Mike hardly slept, he sat there listening to the night noises so he was ready to move at first light. So at sunrise, they were off.

~~~o~~~

Exhaustion had taken its toll on Jack and he slept like the dead that night and his alarm woke him at 5:30 a.m., it was light at 6 and he was on the move. He had no need to sweep up as the ground was so hard, and he was soon on the road back. He had become a bit blasé as to this bumpy track and he was back on the tarmac in less than a few hours. As soon as his wheels hit the tarmac, he was away like greased lightning. With his foot hard down on the accelerator, he managed to get back to near Tawrirt and turned off, he stopped for a rest, a coffee and a hot meal. It was soon dark again, so he settled down again for the night, he couldn't sleep much, but was able to listen to the portable radio he had brought with him. He had a restless night and was pleased to see the changing light. He was back in his car and away. Traffic was building up and he was forced to overtake often.

Jack carried on along the N6 until he reached Mohammidia, then the A1 and the N1 back to Algiers. He had a couple of hours before dark and drove to the sea and along until he found a reasonable hotel. He parked the 4x4 and went to the reception, where he took a room for the night. He went to the room and stripped off and got underneath the shower – it appeared that he had brought a lot of the desert back with him. He put on clean clothes, and walked down to a nice outside area with swimming pool and bar. He ordered a large cold lager and drank that down quickly and ordered another one.

Jack rang the airport to book the earliest possible flight. He was lucky in that they had a cancellation and he could get a plane at 11 a.m. the next morning. He said that he would get there early, but wouldn't be able to get there three hours before, they said that as long as he was there with one and a half hours before take-off, he would be okay.

He went to dinner early as he was so hungry and fortunately, it was a buffet-style meal, so he helped himself to a large portion. Having eaten, he went to an indoor bar and had a couple more beers, then eventually he went upstairs to bed. His head had hardly touched the pillow and he was asleep.

~~~0~~~

He drove up to another road which was pretty good and they were able to get some speed up. Three hours later, Mike came to a small track off the road; they were off-road now so slow progress was made but all of a sudden they were there. Mike jumped out, checked the compass again and quickly worked out the runway. and where the petrol and supplies were to be buried. They were getting good and quick at this and they were sorted and Mike was back behind the wheel in an hour and a half.

He drove back onto the road, they had tied some brush behind them to try to rubout their tracks. Ben jumped out and removed the brush and off they went. Another six hours, and Mike drove off of the main roads and drove to another clearing about two miles away. This clearing had quite a few large stones across which he moved by hand and raked the surface to create a flat place to land. He marked the places where he wanted to hide the petrol supplies whilst Donald and Ben dug holes and buried the supplies. Then he put in the lights and transponder.

"Can we help?"

"No, I must do this job, go and relax I won't be long."

"Suit yourself."

It took him longer than he thought it would, but at last, he was finished. He went back and climbed back into the Land Rover. Although he needed to rest, he had to drive to the last site. He drank some water and then started up and drove back onto the main road.

"Wow, that was a hot one," he said driving as fast as he could which in the Land Rover wasn't that fast. He got to the point where he turned off the road and went off-road at 10 miles an hour, and reached the clearing with less than an hour before it got dark. They jumped out, Mike quickly took a compass bearing and took stock of what they needed to do.

They got the petrol cans out, there were twice as many this time and also they had to bury the extra fuel tanks that had to be put on the aircraft, as well as a spare parts cache with oil filters and other necessities.

They did what they could, really just making ready for the morning.

"The van is empty now."

"Yes, when we finish here, that's it, back home we go."

"We've just got to fill up the Land Rover as well."

They sat around the primus stove and ate well and had a couple of bottles of cold beer, then settled down to sleep for an early start in the morning.

~~o~~

Jack woke up at about 9:00, had some breakfast, went back to his room and checked he had everything and went to reception to check out. He went out to the sand-covered 4x4, gave the seat a quick brush off and drove to the airport. He handed the car keys back in and went to the check-in desk where he had to follow the same procedure that he had at Gatwick. He went into the duty-free concourse bought himself some coffee and found himself a seat.

~~o~~

As soon as Mike awoke, he was out of the van and busy smoothing the landing surface. Ben and Donald were soon after him and digging holes for the tanks and other stuff. It did not take them long and by the time they had filled everything in and marked the spots, Mike had put the lighting in, finished putting in the transponder and tested it out. It all worked okay.

He staggered back to the Land Rover and found that Donald had already tied some brushwood to the back.

"Great."

They were ready, Mike took a long slug of water and off they went. He drove to the main road, checked it was clear and Ben got out quickly and removed the brushwood and off they went. He took the road back to the border in the same place where they had come from the day before, they could possibly have crossed the border earlier, but Donald and Ben were unsure of the terrain. It was also rumoured that the border was being patrolled.

This was a much longer way to go and it was six hours later that they reached the border point, Ben and Donald jumped out and Mike went through the check-point. He drove down the road and waited in a lay by, Donald and Ben joined him and they drove back to the hotel. He dropped them off where he had picked them up.

"I'll pay you when I see you at the beach, but I'm having a shower first."

"Okay, we will be there in about an hour and a half."

He went back through the hotel security gate parked up and went to his room. He jumped into the shower, got out and took out the money he had smuggled into the country he counted out the $1000 then went to the bar for a few cold beers.

He walked down to the beach, Ben and Donald were there and he beckoned them over. Shook hands, and handed them a couple of ice-cold beers.

"Cheers," he said.

They were some ways from anyone, so he gave Ben the package of money.

"Thanks for that, wasn't too bad, was it?"

"No, not bad at all."

He took out his phone and made a text to Jack.

All done my end.

There was nothing else he could do but worry that Jack was okay and it had all gone well.

~~~o~~~

It wasn't very long before his flight was called and along with the other passengers went to the gate and boarded. He settled himself down for the flight, he did not have a window seat and was seated next to two men in Arabic dress. He didn't care where he sat, he just wanted to get off the ground and back to the UK.

On and off he slumbered his way back to Gatwick. The plane landed with no problems and taxied to its allotted station. He got off with the others from his plane and walked down the corridors to the turntables where he lost no time in collecting his luggage and passing through customs, on to the station, and was lucky that after a few minutes he got on a train to Clapham Junction.

Having got there, he had to wait for about 20 minutes, then the train arrived and he got on and found himself a seat and a couple of hours later, he was back home. Just before he got there, he rang his mother to pick him up. She was very pleased to see him safe.

Mike arrived back just a few days before, he gave Jack a big hug and then got back in the driving seat. Jack jumped in the passenger side and they drove off.

"Welcome home, did everything go okay?"

"Yes, everything's in place. I'll tell you about it tomorrow."

"Okay."

Mike was pleased to get home, he had arrived home the same day but, in the evening, and rang Veronica to pick him up as well, have a shower and settle down to sleep in his own bed. He went out like a light and woke refreshed in the morning. He got up showered and dressed and went down to breakfast, Cornflakes.

Jack was out in the garden.

"Let you sleep in but are you ready to go over everything now?"

"After you've made a cup of coffee."

"Okay."

Mike made the coffee and came back out with the two mugs and sat down.

He already had his own Garmin out so that they could swap coordinates so that they both had the exact position of the landing sites. They swapped stories of the problems and journeys that they had made.

They were nearly ready, or at least a good portion was sorted out. They had nearly done the preparation.

Next thing was to get the microlight near to where they needed it. To this end, they had to dismantle it so that they could have it flown to a warehouse. They chose one that was on the airfield, as this was a small airport it was locked up at night with no guards and plenty of old unused buildings on it.

They had it boxed up and collected with Mike's name as the customer so that all he had to do was to collect it at the airport.

~~~o~~~

Veronica prepared for her trip to Berithroa and the court where Deb was to be tried. It would have looked very odd if her mother had not been there to support her, and she had managed to get permission to see her for a while. Before or after the trial.

Her flight was early the next morning and Jack would take her to the airport. So she would get there the day before in readiness.

If she was convicted then it was her job to let Mike know when the prison van left. Then get out of the country as quickly as possible.

~~~o~~~

Mike took a direct flight, he had not booked a hotel but as the flight was overnight, he hoped to get some sleep on the plane.

On arrival, he went to the warehouse where his microlight was stored. He had hired a small car, and he had put three five-gallon containers of petrol in the boot.

He went into the office and asked to collect it, they showed him where it was. He asked if he could borrow a pallet truck to take it out of the compound and move it out of the way, and of course would pay for the privilege, but wanted to check that it had arrived okay. With suitable payment it was fine, so he used the pallet truck and one by one he took the boxes out of the store and to where he could open them to check them out. Then took the pallet truck back. He opened the main and heaviest container and quickly undid the quick release clamps that he and Jack had used, then pulled it out of the container and behind a wall of a disused warehouse, then quickly disassembling the container, hiding that as well, removing the invoice panel.

He then did the same with the other carton which contained the wings and the fundamental stuff needed such as oil. He removed the petrol from the boot and then drove the car out and handed the keys in.

He went back to the disused warehouse by foot and set about assembling the machine and last of all finishing by adding the oil and then petrol. He then sat back and waited till the airport closed and the light began to fade, then he pressed the starter, she fired up on his fourth attempt.

He shut her down again as he didn't want to leave till it was completely dark.

Night came suddenly, and he put on his flying gear and helmet, switched on the ignition and steered himself out from behind the wall. He had everything ready as he would be flying by instruments to his destination.

He hit the gas and off he went, the little plane was quickly air-born and he revelled in the sweet sound of the engine, and turned her away from passing directly over the roads; of course, he had no lights on at all. He set her on her course and away they went. He had to keep quite low as he didn't want to be seen on the radar so he had to concentrate.

After several hours, he was getting very close to his destination and the most dangerous part for him. The moonlight helped and occasionally he caught a glimpse of the tarmac road below, the sat nav showed him that he was fast approaching the sharp bend which was the ambush point.

He shut down the engine and glided down towards the road, he needed to land before the bend. Lower and lower he glided and he put on his landing lights and landed turning off his lights straight away.

He quickly got out and pushed the little machine into the gap in the bush he had found in the Land Rover and did his best to camouflage it as much as possible, he would check it again in daylight

He dug up the petrol cans and filled the tank up on the little craft.

Jack arrived home and grabbed his bags and supplies and was straight out down to the microlight airfield where he boarded his craft, he had been hiring this one for a while and they offered it to him cheap as he was a member, and they wanted to get a newer model. He took off and set his course for Shoreham. All parts of the rescue were now mobilised.

Mike having camouflaged the craft, sat in the cockpit and snuggled into his flight gear and tried to get to sleep. Early next morning, he checked out his attempt to hide his craft and thought it was okay and settled down for a cold breakfast. It was going to be a long day. He waited for the prison van to pass as he wanted to see what it looked like, see how many guards were in it and he needed to see if it was armoured.

About 11 a.m. he heard an engine and got in a good position to see it go by. He was relieved to see it was an ordinary minibus with two warders in it and he got a slight glimpse at Deb. Now he had to wait for a signal from Veronica, that they were on their way back and whether to go ahead with the rescue.

~~~o~~~

Veronica was in tears when she saw Deb, she had lost so much weight but she waved at her and Deb who was looking around the court saw her.

She was escorted and handcuffed to a warder into the dock.

The charges were read out and the evidence submitted. The defence didn't really say anything and the judge just indicated that she was guilty as charged. There was no jury, and she was sentenced to 10 years. Veronica couldn't believe it had happened so quickly and cried hysterically as did Deb. Her solicitor asked the judge whether Deb's mother could visit her and the judge granted her a half-hour slot before they left for prison.

There was a lot of crying and hugging when the warder let them. Veronica tried to console her, telling her that she would be fighting for her through the British Government.

Then Veronica was asked to leave, and waited outside to see the van off then phoned Mike.

"Do it," she said, "leaving now."

Then she went to the airport to book her flight and managed to get one in an hour.

~~~o~~~

Mike had plenty of time but wanted to be ready so he took out the stinger and ran it across the road shovelling leaves over it, it was a type that when he pulled a wire on it the spikes sprang up. So any vehicle passing over it before he deployed it would pass safely.

He had some plastic cable ties which were already put into loops like handcuffs so all he needed to do was to pull the ends and they would tighten up.

He sat back in the plane and relaxed as much as he could. he had worked out roughly how long it would take them to reach the prison and was ready.

It was some hours when he heard an engine in the distance and prepared to act quickly. He readied his bow, slung his quiver full of arrows over his shoulder. The van came towards the bend and was going quite fast. He deployed the stinger quickly, the van went across it and it took out all four tyres. The driver completely lost control and the van went straight off the road, hit a concealed bank and rolled over onto its back.

Mike didn't wait any longer, as soon as the van had gone past him, he had chased it down with the cable ties in his hand, he dropped his bow on a soft cushion of shrubs as he went. As he got to it, one of the wardens was struggling out of a door. He wasted no time slipping the loops onto the warden's hands and pulling them tightly, then ran around the van in time to intercept the other warden and did the same, he checked the van in case there was anyone else other than Deb then fastened cable ties to their feet as well then dragged them together and tied them together. They were in no condition to offer resistance.

He quickly retrieved the keys from the guards although to him with trembling hands he felt clumsy and slow. He opened the side door of the prison van calling her name. Whilst he did, there was no answer.

He grabbed her quickly and pulled her near to the door and using the keys he unlocked the hand and ankle cuffs that secured her. She sighed so he did not need to check her pulse but managed to lift her onto his shoulder. He noticed how light she was, a bonus in a way, as he managed to move quickly across the road. He quickly retrieved his bow and disappeared into the bushes, he managed to trip only twice but not enough to floor him.

He heard another van or something coming down the hill, screeching brakes, and then raised voices, this spurred him on and they got to where the little aircraft stood in readiness, twisting Deb round so that he could drop her into the seat and strap her in.

He started the engine, and heard shouts behind him, he revved the engine up and raced through the gap in the hedge and out along the road. He put the lights on to simulate that he was driving. The craft soon sped up and he lifted off the ground, as gunfire sounded behind him and bullets passed close to the craft, he kept her low and aimed to put a tree between them and the gunfire, two or three bullets had passed through the canopy of the craft and he could hear the wind whistle through them. He hoped that they would not begin to tear. He hoped that he was out of range and began to make some height so that he wouldn't hit a tree on a ridge. Deb still remained silent and in a way that helped him keep all of his attention on the plane.

He adjusted his position on to the course he had planned on earlier and using his electronic gadgetry centred on his first stop for fuel and a place that he could take some time out to get himself and Deb into a comfortable position, as necessity had made him rush to get away from the area.

He checked his position on the navigation equipment as well as his altitude again. He knew that he had about an hour's flying before he could land.

He made some checks and found that all was okay and his course was correct. He was grateful for a clear night, and although there was no moon, the stars afforded him a small degree of light to fly by, but he was completely dependent on his instruments.

Nearer and nearer to the landing point he came and he made his landing checks, he pressed the button on his consul which turned on the guide lights, hopefully. They shone out immediately and he manoeuvred the little craft slightly to align her. He brought her down gently turning on his landing light at the same time. The wheels touched and he came to a stop quickly.

He turned off the engine and lights quickly. Using his torch, he quickly started his fire and using some brushwood to remove the marks that his landing had made. He went to his fuel canister and dug it up and poured the fuel into the craft's fuel tank through a filter to keep out any detritus and sand.

He checked on Deb and found her still unconscious, he checked her pulse, which was steady. He fitted the flight helmet on her head and plugged it into the intercom. He had one more flight to do that night to get them further away from possible pursuit and nearer to the exit from the country. The problem with this next point was the wind, it was head-on and very fast, it buffeted the little craft and he had to constantly battle to not only keep on course, but also to keep her from falling out of the sky. This also meant that she was using fuel far faster than he had catered for, and although he thought that he had planned for the worst, fuel was now critical.

This next landing place was an island surrounded by seawater in an estuary. He had felt this would be a good place as he could see all around him for any sort of problem coming his way. The island was mainly sand but flat, and he lit the runway lights that he had installed previously.

The island was in sight and he aimed the little craft at the landing point crossed his fingers and prepared to land. Suddenly, all went quiet as the engine decided that petrol fumes were no longer sufficient to keep the craft up and the engine went dead.

Even though he was expecting it, it still came as a shock causing him to grip tighter on the controls causing the little craft to rock badly from side to side. He told himself not to panic and managed to relax his grip slightly, but the absence of the engine noise and the wind whistling through the bullet holes and frame attacked his fraught nerves. Then he concentrated on the lights and manoeuvred the craft to the left of centre on them and then realised he was too high he put the nose down hard. If he overshot, he would end up in the water and that would be an end to it.

He touched down, the craft nearly turning over as it hit the ground with one wheel, bouncing around until finishing up 90 degrees to the direction in which he had been coming in from.

He slumped back in his seat letting out a massive sigh of relief.

He quickly unstrapped himself and climbed from the cockpit his legs finding difficulty supporting him as they were shaking so much.

He unstrapped Debbie and half dragged and half carried her to a nearby dune and made her as comfortable as he could. He went to a spring and filled his canteen with the clear sweet water, returned and lifting back her head let some of the water trickle into her mouth.

He took out the lightweight canopy and pegged it over the plane, it was well camouflaged. As it matched well with the sand around them. Quickly checking over the microlight, he was relieved to find no other damage than the three bullet holes. He lit the fire and heated water for some tea. He didn't feel like eating, he just felt drained from the experiences he had had that day.

He took out his repair kit from one of the storage pockets in the little craft and using scissors from his tool kit cut some pieces of repair fabric. He tore off the self-adhesive backing and pressed them into place either side of the bullet holes. That would stop the holes from fraying and tearing.

~~~o~~~

Debbie woke up in the early hours thirsty and needing to attend to the call of nature. She lay still for a minute wondering where she was. Her mind was in turmoil. In her confused state, she was still in her cell with the rats and other creepy crawlies. The guards would soon be coming for her and as the pain came to her, she opened her eyes but it was pitch dark except for the dying embers of the fire. She shivered uncontrollably.

Her father was quickly at her side holding her and reassuring her that everything was all right now and that he was with her. Slowly she began to calm down, her breathing slowing. She grabbed him and cuddled him hard and cried for some while into his shoulder.

She asked him what had happened and how was she with him, how had they got where they were.

"I'll tell you that over dinner," he said, "but I'm not prepared to eat with you until you've had a good bath and washed your hair."

"Are you saying that I smell?" She asked.

"Not really, but to say the least, the perfume you are using is a little on the strong side, and would probably keep any self-respecting skunk away. Come on let me help you up if you can manage it and get you washed and clean."

He handed her a lantern torch and a trowel.

"The toilet is over that dune, do you need a hand?"

"No way," she said with determination.

He helped her up, she gripped her head and swayed dizzily.

"I'll help you to the toilet and leave you for a while, call me when you want and I'll help you to the stream to bathe."

He handed some clean clothes that he had brought for her to change into and sat close by while she washed and helped her back to the microlight. He dug down so that the top of the fuel tank was visible and dug them up. He filled the microlight tank up until it was overflowing, then screwed on the cap and watched the excess fuel evaporate. Deb was fast asleep and he settled down to wait for first light. The stars looked very bright and he hoped that the weather forecast had been correct for today after the unexpected gusts the previous night.

Just before dawn, he detected movement out in the lagoon, it appeared to be a military boat of some type. Although he was loath to do so, he woke Deb from her sleep and gave her a nutritional bar and canteen full of fresh spring water. He helped her into the craft and on with her safety belt, they were ready to fly just as soon as they had to.

As the boat drew nearer, he removed and rolled up the camouflage sheet, packed it away. and the activity of removing the canopy had attracted attention, there was shouting and pointing.

He switched on the ignition and as soon as the engine was running smoothly he opened the throttle. The ground was a little soft and she seemed to stick to the surface but at the last moment, she came unstuck and the game little craft skittered into the sky.

He heard shots pass close by as he swung the craft around the trees and continued in a direction which gave them cover although it was not the direction that he wished to go.

As soon as they were out of range and hopefully out of earshot he looked for somewhere to put down. A small clearing was in sight and he immediately went in to land, he had to trust that the area was clear flat and hard. Luckily it was and he landed without a problem.

It was now inevitable that they would bring in a helicopter to find them now that they had a rough idea in which direction they were headed or thought they had.

Fuel was the most important consideration, and although he had allowed for some latitude for eventualities such as this, he did not have much to waste, He had already nearly crashed from lack of fuel and he didn't want a repeat of that.

He replaced the canopy over the craft and heaped bushes around it to help with camouflage. He left Deb in her seat. He removed his bow from its position on the plane and strapped the arrows and quiver around his waist. It was good that he had pretty good visibility around where they were situated, and he helped Deb down and settled down beneath the canopy. Deb was still half asleep and had no idea what was happening. He had to wait for darkness now to slip away.

Time passed slowly, and the heat was intolerable, at least he had filled the water containers full from the good spring water where they had camped, he quickly buried them to keep them as cool as possible.

Deb was quite dehydrated and hungry when she woke up realising that she was still with her sad. He gave her some water and food rations. She fell back to sleep.

It was early afternoon when they heard the sound of rotors from a helicopter as it flew over them. It was following the course that they had been on when they were last seen from the boat. It slowly disappeared into the distance.

"Could have been better," Mike said, "but could have been a lot worse."

"How long till it gets dark?" asked Debbie.

"About three hours," he replied, "we must be ready to go then."

Deb said that she felt awake enough to keep watch and allow him some sleep. He didn't and couldn't argue.

~~~o~~~

"We must find them, that thing can't carry that much fuel, where would that course lead them, there was nothing seen on radar, so they must have stayed low. Fly to the maximum distance they could have covered, and then move back from there."

They flew back slowly to within 20 miles.

"What now?"

"We need to fly back out but zig-zag as we are going.

"They must have put down somewhere to hide, I'm sure they would not be so naïve to expect no pursuit."

They kept up the search till about 30 minutes before dark, as the helicopter was not allowed to be used at night and they needed to refuel at the nearest base 150 miles away.

"There is no way they're going to fly that thing back to England. So how do they intend to get there? It can only be by plane, but not from this country, it must be a neighbouring country with no extradition treaty. They are not going to fly during the day, they will only move at night, and probably meet up with a car somewhere. We can only fly the helicopter during the day.

"We need to catch them and hunt them down during the day."

~~~o~~~

The Chief Superintendent called Joshua and Zane into his office and told them to shut the door behind them. They sat down as he unrolled a large-scale map of Berithroa.

"I am sure that you have heard about the prison break by now. I have all the details now, at 10:30 in the evening the van carrying a drug smuggler was ambushed, they used a stinger and escaped in a light aircraft.

"The fugitive was released, both of the wardens were injured and restrained using those plastic cable ties."

"How are they?" asked Zane.

"They were taken to hospital, but have been allowed home now."

"They were nearly caught when a patrol boat saw them on an island, they managed to get air-born and the boat lost them. A helicopter was scrambled to find them acting on the course and direction the boat gave. Unfortunately, it had to return to its base for refuelling. We now know that the aircraft is a microlight so only a pilot and the fugitive can be on board. A search for them is still underway as we speak and more officers have been deployed to help.

"Do not look so worried, you two are not part of that, well, not completely anyway. The drug smuggler was caught at the airport with two possible accomplices. We had no evidence against them so they were deported.

"However, South Africa are complaining that a drug shipment still got through to their country from which eight people have already died, so it would appear that these girls were only part of the plot.

"However, you were both at the airport that day as Joshua you were on the same flight coming back from your holidays so you are involved in this case anyway."

"Didn't see any arrest," said Joshua.

The superintendent looked at Zane, "What about you, you were there to pick him up, weren't you?"

"No, nothing."

"Well, it's your case now, we need to get this drug-running stopped completely to get a bit of credit back from the South African Police. So get on it."

"This our main priority."

They left the room and immediately went to their own office, shut the door and sat down with a coffee.

"Right," said Joshua, "let's get a list of what we need to obtain to help us."

"The main thing is to get as much video as possible.

From our customs area

From outside the airport

From customs in Lisbon

From around the duty free at Lisbon

From outside the airport at Lisbon

We also need the details of the fugitive and her accomplices. Also a passenger list for the flight they came in on."

"Right, let's get on and hit the phones."

The first call that Joshua made was to his wife, Wendy. When he told her about the girls she couldn't believe it and remembering back she said that they had been fruit picking for a couple of weeks to get their bank balances up.

"Well, they wouldn't have to do that if they were getting money with a drug cartel. They seemed so nice and natural, they played with the kids and kept them busy for hours, can't see them being criminals."

He had to agree.

He told her that he would be late that evening.

Some of the details were coming in already. The passenger list came through and the video in the customs area. This took a large amount of time as when looking at them they had to watch what else was happening in the hall. He found the part where the girls were entering the customs area and slowed it down because if someone was using them as a distraction then they would want to be going through just after the girls were caught.

He saw the customs officer checking the bags of the first girl. He saw that although she was annoyed at having her belongings scattered across the desk, she accepted it and took her belongings over to a table and repacked. The next girl was Deb, he saw her face accept that she was going to get the same treatment and turn to the last girl and shrug as if to say my turn.

He watched the customs officer who even before he had undone her bags took a furtive glance at a couple passing by and the customs officer at that desk waving them through.

"Suspicious," he said to Zane, "look."

He showed him the video.

"Let's find out who this couple was and where they went," and anything else they could find out.

Also, he wanted details of both of the customs officers both of them.

These enquiries were distributed to other staff by Zane with orders to keep them discrete. They didn't want anyone on their guard for the moment.

Right, it was time to get home or they would never get there.

He asked for an update about the microlight and was told that they hadn't found them yet and the circle of where they could be now merged into other countries.

~~~o~~~

As soon as darkness fell, Mike removed the camouflage and packed it away. He helped Deb into her seat and buckle up then went round and got himself comfortable. He looked at Deb.

"Are you ready?"

"As I'll ever be."

He turned the key and she started on the first time, he switched on both the runway and landing lights, revved up and off they went, a quick start, then up and away.

Deb was awake this time and leaving the ground took her breath away, and she swore.

"Bloody hell."

"Don't swear," her father admonished her, as he turned off the lights.

"Don't be alarmed, we're going to be okay."

He brought her round to the course that he needed to be on. It was nice at first to feel the cold night air but that changed soon enough to freezing cold. They flew for an hour and a half and with relief, he had got to the point where he needed to turn on the concealed lights which showed him the runway. To his joy, he could see them about 30 degrees to his left and turned quickly to line up with them.

He turned on his landing lights and came in to land scattering a few small animals, lizards he thought, as he landed smoothly.

He helped Deb down.

"Have a sit down for a minute, but don't get too comfortable cause we will be off again soon."

He dug a hole for a latrine, helped Deb to it and left her.

He pulled the plane back to the take-off position, and filled the tanks from his hidden store, did his pre-flight checks and was ready.

She staggered back to her seat. Mike helped her in and gave her some water and something to eat, then he got in himself, started the engine, and off they went again.

They were soon up and away, Mike brought the little plane on to her course.

"We need to get the hell out of this country, and tonight would be good."

"How many more stops have we to make?"

"Two including this one, then we will be across the border and safer."

"How do you mean safer, is that not the end of our Journey?"

"No! but I cannot talk further, I need to concentrate, we are flying quite low."

After about another 90 minutes, Mike brought her in to land again, so far so good. Again, Mike dragged the machine back to where it was ready to take off again.

"Is there anything that I can do to help?" Deb asked. "Yes, get the water bottles filled to the brim."

"Drink plenty, but remember we cannot stop on this Journey."

He filled the tank up with fuel. Then he went across to where he had buried the extra tanks. He dug them up and then fitted them to the plane. It had taken him longer than he had hoped.

At last, he had them fitted, then he filled them with fuel. He opened a valve which turned them on. He motioned Deb to get back in. He checked her safety belt and prepared for take-off.

She started straight away, he looked at his watch it was later than he thought, but he considered that it was just doable but with a bit of extra risk, but being across the border was so magnetic and would be a relief to get out of this accursed land.

He revved her up hard because of the extra weight of fuel and they were off, the plane seemed stuck for a few moments, and he felt panic creep up on him. Then gradually, she became unstuck and they were off the ground, just.

They were not very high, and Mike knew that they had to get higher to get over the mountains. It seemed that now that they were off the ground, the plane could climb well and started to get higher, but he didn't want to climb too quickly or they would be seen on the radar.

It was difficult to see the mountains at night but after half an hour they could see that the ground was getting rockier. Mike could see reasonably well due to the starlight. They began to ascend slowly in tune with the gradient, but Mike knew that very soon he would have to climb high and quickly.

They reached the start of the mountains at last. He climbed hard and up she went, at last, they got to the highest part, the little craft faltered slightly and began to run rough due to the thin air and both he and Deb were finding it a little harder to breathe.

Mike explained what was happening, and explained that it would change soon.

He manoeuvred the craft between the peaks of the mountain and after 30 minutes, the mountains disappeared, and he could bring the craft down. The engine picked up and it was easier to breathe and on they went. The ground had changed, rockier, harder looking and on they went.

Alarmed, Mike noticed not only the sandy landscape but that he was seeing it a little clearer, he looked at his watch and realised that he was not going to get to his next landing point until the sun was up.

It was getting much lighter and it was a relief for him to see from his instruments that he was not far off, and turned on the runway lights.

He came in to land and touched down with a bounce but quickly slowed and stopped.

Mike unstrapped himself and quickly covered up the plane with his camouflage canopy, but this time he used the underside out which was a sand colour pattern.

Deb helped and they covered the edges in loose sand. Mike was knackered, his eyes felt like lead, Deb managed to get some brushwood and started a fire to make some tea.

"Wow, that's good," Mike said, "even without milk."

He closed his eyes and drifted off to sleep.

~~~o~~~

Next morning, Joshua was at his desk bright and early but not as early as Zane.

He was looking through the video now in from Lisbon regarding the duty-free area. He watched the antics and movements of the two girls, they were just enjoying themselves like everybody else.

Next, he checked the video of outside the airport and saw the girls sitting in the seating area chatting and drinking coffee, then another couple came and sat down near them, he backtracked it slightly and saw the slight imperceptible nod at them by the woman.

He carried on watching as the man got up and bought a coffee for himself and his wife and the girls put all the bags in a pile near them. The girls then went to the shops.

He couldn't see all the details but could see that the woman was going down one of the bags and the man passed her a package and the woman did up the bag, then they carried on drinking their coffee and eating.

The girls came back, picked up their bags deposited them and went through to duty free, and then a little while later the couple got up and with their bags, went back out of the airport.

He called Joshua and showed him the film, they managed to get good close up of the couple.

"Well, the three girls were set up nicely and now two of them have been deported and one is on the run."

"Whoever got them out had nothing to do with a drug cartel, so it must be someone the family had hired."

In the meantime, he went to see the Superintendent to cancel the search for them. It was just a waste of resources to carry it on. The Chief Superintendent agreed and got straight on the phone.

~~~o~~~

The heat woke him up, he looked at his watch, it was midday and he had a lot to do. He turned on his phone for the first time since he had entered the country.

He texted to Jack, *All okay*. This was the code that he was out of Berithroa. He received a reply, *Okay*, so that he knew that Jack had received his message.

He turned off the phone as they could give away his position.

He stripped to the waist as it was so hot and went to where there was a spanner laying on the sand, a quick dig around revealed a box of spare parts for the plane. He had to change parts to give the plane a service, oil filter, spark plugs air filter, battery and other parts. It took him about an hour at which point he stopped and waited for the sun to move down in the sky and the temperature to drop slightly.

The other thing he did was to check that his phone was fully charged, he didn't have to check by turning it on, he had a charging point on the plane and checked that there was a charge getting from the battery, it was okay.

He filled up the system with oil, and then with fuel with the extra tanks. His range was now conservatively 180 miles and he looked forward to reaching the next point in their escape. He refilled all the water containers they had. If they did have any trouble, then this water had to last them until rescue.

It started to get dark at about 5:45 and was fully dark by 6:00 p.m. He was feeling a bit better for the rest and he motioned Deb to get into her seat and fix the seat belt, which he checked. They were ready to go. He folded and rolled the camouflage canopy and placed it in its holder, he then made certain that he had left nothing behind and everything he had used but was not taking with him was buried.

He had already swept the tracks where he had landed but was well aware that he would make more on take-off. He turned the key. The engine fired and settled to a nice idle, as with most engines, she preferred running in the cool air and sounded sweet as a nut. He revved her up and off they went straight and level for the next landing spot in about three hours' time.

There was a crescent moon which gave the terrain they were flying over an eerie quality, but at the same time comforting. After flying for about an hour, he spotted some tents and camels tethered, and swung the little craft to avoid them, they had a fire and he could see people looking up to the sky to see what was making a noise in the peace of the desert. As soon as he was out of sight and out of hearing range of them, he resumed his course.

He looked at his instruments and he navigated for the landing which was 20 miles away from his direct course just to throw any pursuers off the scent.

On approach to his next landing point, he circled the area to make certain that it was clear before he switched on the lights and came into land smoothly. He jumped out quickly and gave Deb the shovel, as she went to walk into the shadows he said smiling, "Watch out for the scorpions and snakes," and saw her come back and take the lantern light with her.

He laughed.

"Thanks for that."

"Just hurry up, we don't want to be too long."

Once again he saw a spanner on the ground. This was the sign that the fuel was there and he quickly uncovered the top and filled the tanks up. He wondered what it was that he had uncovered in a bag beside it. Deb looked over his shoulder, it was a bag of coffee with powdered milk, some biscuits and a note which read:

IF YOU HAVE TIME

"Brother Jack, you are a star," she said "We do have time, don't we? It will help you keep awake."

"Too right."

They found that firewood and kindling had also been left for them. They lit the fire and made the coffee, it tasted great along with the biscuits he had left them. They put out the fire, covered their tracks as best they could and took their places ready for take-off. Mike took out the phone and texted:

Thanks, we needed that.

Okay, he got back.

He switched off the phone They took off again.

Mike knew that he could not afford to be complacent and he made himself concentrate, the coffee helped greatly, but he was tiring quickly.

He said to Deb, "I'm absolutely knackered, so keep an eye out all around for any sign of habitation or anything that points to people being around."

She watched out but she was tired as well but couldn't see anyone.

The terrain was changing now and Mike brought the craft higher as the surface was going from rocks and fairly even ground to more sand with dunes forming.

Mike knew that the landing strip they sought was among these dunes and just hoped that it wasn't too covered by sand, but he hadn't realised just how high these dunes were so had to climb higher to receive a homing signal but not too high, he didn't want to get pipped on the radar.

Eventually, he came to the point where he should be able to see the landing site and pressed the light switch, sure enough, they were heading directly for it. The fact that the lights were showing told him the sand level was okay, showing that he could go on to a second landing strip. The second landing was safer for landing but far less safe in regard to being caught, they may have escaped from the country where Deb had been held, but they were now in a country they had no papers for and this country would have no hesitation in sending them both back.

He landed smoothly with a large sigh of relief. Deb helped him move the plane back to its take-off position and spread the canopy over her and push sand over the edge to help keep it concealed and make it secure and feel safe.

He opened his phone and made the text: *Arrived safely.*

Okay, he received.

He turned the phone off again.

They took turns with the shovel and on return, they laid down and went to sleep immediately. He knew that they should have kept guard overnight, but he was just too damned tired.

Fortunately, the camouflage canopy was pretty good and they would be all but invisible. During the morning there was a sudden gust of wind and a couple of minutes later a full-scale sand storm.

Fortunately, they were in the lea of some large dunes which gave them some protection but that did not stop the sand from moving down the dunes and covering the camp in several inches of sand. Mike and Deb had both woken up at the start.

"What's that, what's happening?" Called out a worried Deb.

"Don't panic," said Mike, "this will make it better for us, no one will see us now."

The sand storm lasted about two hours and the covering blotted out all the light beneath the canopy, so they made the most of it and got a few more hours of sleep. Mike had ached a bit from sleeping where he had but now felt good.

"Make yourself comfortable girl, the sand we are on is soft so move your body around till it moulds to your shape and you should be comfortable."

Mike woke up a couple of hours later, he was a bit muzzy headed but also refreshed, boy had he needed that sleep. He looked at the time on his watch and realised that it would be dark again in a couple of hours. They had a lot to do the biggest of which was going to be clearing the runway of loose sand. He quickly sorted out the refilling and pre-flight checks as he could manage them beneath the canopy. He burrowed out beneath the edge of the canopy, making a small hole to look through, all seemed quiet so he enlarged it till he could get out.

Deb followed him out. The little campsite was all but invisible, which was good, but there was a lot of sand over the small runway that had to be removed the wind however had cleared most of it and it had built up the next dune noticeably.

He took out his folding shovel and using the edge, scraped away the new sand. He knew how quickly the sun went down here, so he and Deb quickly packed everything into the plane, the canopy took some pulling away from the sand which had trapped the sides, but they got it out and folded and rolled it up placing it into its holder.

The darkness came down and the plane went up. Mike took the craft a little higher to avoid the dunes. He took her on to the course he chose and cruised along for about two hours, then he turned on the runway lights once more and brought her down switching on his landing lights. He smiled to himself as he landed, this was the last night flight and the last low-level flight as well.

Tonight was going to be a pleasant evening as long as they could keep hidden till morning. He and Deb followed the procedure that they had become used to. And as soon as they had hidden the plane, he filled up the tanks and gave the plane another really good check and service, new plugs filters and oil.

He walked round to the side of a dune where a motorcycle was parked up with two crash helmets. He smiled and went back to the camp laughing.

"Come on you sod, tell me what is happening."

He laughed again and taking his shovel out again dug up where although Deb had not seen it but there was a sign like a coat hanger on the ground, he dug down and retrieved a sealed bag and delving inside found two bags of clothing including trainers. He looked inside and tossed one bag to Deb. She looked inside and shrieked as it had fresh clothes for her, but she was a little bewildered at what clothing there was.

"Just a bit of a disguise, don't put them on yet."

"Hell," she said, "I could do with a shower before I do."

"Yes, we both could," he said and handed her a kit bag.

"Put them in here," he said, putting his own clothes in.

"Come on."

He led her to where the motorbike was and tossed her one of the helmets.

"Where are we going?"

"You'll see."

He got on and started the bike up and motioned her to get on the back.

It was obvious that he had no intention of explaining anything.

He drove down a track and onto the road, then he turned left and drove for about an hour until they came to a hotel. She saw the sign *The Arabian Night lodge hotel*. He turned into it and parked the bike in the main car park.

"Follow my lead, okay," he said.

"Okay," she said bewildered.

They passed through some automatic opening doors, and Mike walked to the lift and pressed the button for the 4th floor. He walked down the corridor till he came to room 453, he took a card that had been in his section of stuff in the bag, placed it over the lock and the lock opened. He went in with Deb following. He pointed to the bathroom, gave her the clothes and said, "There you are, fill your boots. I'll be on the balcony."

Deb went in and locked the door. There was a bath and a shower everything was a luxury; there was shampoo, soap, toothpaste and brush, everything.

She stripped off her clothes and got under the shower, the water was as hot as she could stand. She scrubbed her hair and body twice.

Then she filled the bath also as hot as she could stand and got in sinking up to her neck, there was bubble bath as well and she stayed in there for ages until the water had cooled somewhat.

Then she dried and dressed puzzled with the choice of trouser suit, but what the heck, Dad would explain sometime.

She cleaned her teeth twice as well.

She exited the bathroom, as she supposed somewhat guiltily that she ought to let her father have his turn. He was out on the balcony reading a UK newspaper. He got up and smiled at her

"Better?"

"Not many," she said.

He took his turn in the bathroom, shaving with a disposable razor, and a nice hot shower. He was in there all of 40 minutes and came out wearing a similar outfit. She could see that the logo on the back was the same as hers with *Jacks Microlight Flights of Fancy* written on it and the picture of a microlight aircraft on it.

"I guess I should explain," he said. "We are flying from here to London across Europe as quickly as possible. You are the photographer, I am the pilot."

He handed her a copy of a map, so that if asked she knew where they were going.

"Right," he said. "Dinner and more importantly drinks, and ice-cold ones."

"How did you arrange all of this?" she asked.

"I didn't," he said, "Jack did."

They went down to the dining room where they picked up plates and helped themselves to the buffet. The food was very good, they ordered drinks; she had a large gin and tonic, he had an ice-cold lager.

The first one didn't touch the sides and he was soon on his second. It was getting late now so they went into the dining room and helped themselves to the buffet, then went back to the room and retrieved the bag filled now with the old clothes they had arrive with. They went downstairs, they didn't need to do any more than drop off the door lock card. Everything else had been paid for, even the drinks.

They went back to the bike and he drove them back to the camp where he turned on the phone, his own phone which had also been in the bag. They laid down and slept till morning light.

They were woken by the phone ringing.

"Hi," said Jack, "will be with you in an hour and a half will you be ready?"

"Yes, see you soon. We'll rendezvous as planned okay."

"Yes."

He rang off.

Deb was awake.

"Was that Jack? I wanted to say hello."

"You are not supposed to be here, and you never know who is listening."

"Come on, let's get her ready to fly."

They took off the tarpaulin and Mike re-checked that everything was okay. He went back to where everything had been buried. He took out another bag and from that removed two life jackets, he handed Deb one.

"Get that on you, but hopefully, we won't need it, it's not too far, and we can fly a bit higher than we have been. There's a camera here, you are the photographer, so you'd better carry one and an identification card. I know you have no passport, but you don't need one in Europe. Let me check your life jacket is on correctly, just to be safe. To fill it you just have to pull this little handle, same as they tell you when you fly. Remember don't inflate it until you are in the water."

~~~o~~~

Joshua and Zane didn't let the grass grow under their feet. They sent colleagues out to arrest the two customs officers. Whilst that was being done, Joshua rang a contact in the Lisbon Police Department and asked for some help, he sent pictures to them of the couple at the airport and the couple who had passed through customs stayed at a local hotel for a couple of days and returned to Lisbon. He explained his interest in them.

It didn't take too long, he was called by a member of the Portuguese drug squad with the news that they had identified all the people in the photographs. They talked about what the people had been up to and it was agreed that the Portuguese squad would carry on with the investigation at their end.

~~~o~~~

"Right, lets board, we have to take off in 10 minutes precisely."

"Why?"

"You'll see, but we must be punctual its part of our cover."

He turned the key and revved the engine, she sounded sweet. Off they went down the runway, he was revving hard, she lifted off and away they went, he gained some height and moved on to his course.

They flew over a town and then in the distance was the sea, on they went till they were over the shore. Mike had turned on the radio receiver that had been in the spares for the plane.

Suddenly:

"Tally Ho, Tally Ho," they heard and a wild, "whoop."

With that another microlight appeared on the right-hand side and Jack waved to them, and they waved back.

"Is the filming okay?" he said.

Deb replied, "Yes, no problem, but I need to use a wide-angle lens."

"Why? To get your ego in?"

They all laughed and Mike had to tell them to keep it serious. He smiled to himself though, he was so relieved they were together again, he could almost cry.

It was next stop, Spain.

Jack came over the radio, "Look at the ships, this is a very busy shipping lane, and it's only about ten miles wide."

Deb looked and before they had completely lost contact with the Tunisian coast, they were in sight of the Spanish coast. They had to skirt around Gibraltar and land in Spain.

They had a good view of Gibraltar as they went around it. The reason for giving it a clear birth being that there was an international airport there and that it was a military area. Mike explained that when planes land or take off from there, they have to close the main road to Spain as it goes across the flight path. Also, the rock is susceptible to strong winds, not good for flying microlights comfortably.

It was far less demanding flying at a good altitude, and it was comforting to have Jack on his wing, but they still had to keep their eyes peeled, but they had clearance to fly to Casarrubios Airfield, near Madrid, but had to keep to the flight plan that had been accepted. Jack was in contact with the flight controllers and would relay any deviation necessary to Mike via his radio.

Jack came on the radio to change course to 230 which they slowly did, this brought them on course for landing. Ahead in the distance, Mike could see another aircraft doing the same.

"Descend to 1000 feet," he said. And they started to come down, they could see the little airport now and turning into the wind came in to land. Jack went first, and Mike slowed to give him plenty of room then landed behind him, and followed him to where they were to park.

They climbed out and walked to meet each other, but Mike warned them, no sign of emotion as the fuel truck was coming towards them and a customs car. Jack took charge of filling up their tanks, whilst Mike looked after the customs officer who looked quickly over the microlights, but as they were staying on the airport and leaving next day didn't concern himself with them too much. He explained that their bags would be scrutinised when they left the airport and when they came back.

They went through the customs area in the little airport terminal and hired a taxi to go to a nice little restaurant. Here they could be themselves and before they went in, Mike and Jack exchanged hugs and Deb and Jack enjoyed big emotional ones. Mike supplied Deb with a tissue to dry her eyes. Then they entered and ordered breakfast with fresh orange juice and cups of coffee, read the papers and chatted.

Breakfast was a large roll with tomato and ham with olive oil.

"You've lost a bit of weight," Jack said, "but not where you needed to."

"Where's that," Deb asked indignantly. "I didn't need to lose any weight."

"Yes, you did. Your Head", he laughed. Whilst the siblings carried on with their banter, Mike went outside and used his phone, after a while, he got his connection through to Veronica. He hoped that she would remember not to mention Deb or what they had been doing. He needn't have worried.

"At last," she said, "I've been so worried about you, Jack let me know that you were okay, but I've been longing to hear your voices, how did she fly."

"Well, very well. These charity trips take an age, but hell I've missed you, and I will be home soon I hope, all's fine here and we're in Spain, so see you soon," said Mike.

They took off again in the morning sun from the airfield and proceeded on their flight plan, stopping to refuel at Pamplona Airfield Nth Spain

Agers La Garenne Airport near Bordeau

Nantes Atlantique Airport

Carpignet Airport

Calais-Dunkerque Airport

Lydd Aero Club

And Shoreham Airport UK

They took off from Shoreham Airport at 2:00 p.m. sharp, obviously looking forward to getting home. Deb could not wait to sleep in her own bed, luxury that would certainly be. They carried on flying over the South Downs. They could see people walking, and working there. So picturesque. England may not be the warmest country they had been through, but it was beautiful, and definitely the most welcoming.

They had to keep their eyes peeled around Basingstoke and on towards Popham as there were so many low flying military helicopters around. They joined the landing circuit and at last, took their turn to land one at a time. It was a grass airport but had been used for ages. The plane seemed to know its way and they landed smoothly and taxied to the Club parking position.

Both Mike and Jack patted their little craft and thanked them for safe journeys home. Deb gave the plane a kiss of sincere thanks for getting her home.

She just hoped that they couldn't extradite her back.

They went into the Club House and Mike went straight to the bar, he ordered some drinks to celebrate and some food to eat. They were all suddenly very hungry. Jack's car was still parked there so they loaded all their gear into it then got in and went home.

It was a couple of days later that she and Jack were talking that she realised the risk and cost of the rescue, and felt really bad. Jack comforted her, "Look at the bright side, both Dad and I are the fittest we've ever been. Dad has a new career, He now works at Popham as a microlights salesman, Training instructor as Ron has taken him on as a partner as he was finding it too much.

"It would have been the same if it had been me imprisoned. He would have still tried the rescue, and you would have given your best as I have, the only difference is that you would probably have got me hanged.

"We are a tighter family now than we have ever been."

She felt better for that, and went and cuddled her parents in tears.

"What's the matter?" asked Veronica, alarmed.

"Nothing," she said, "but thanks for being my mum and dad," and gave them a kiss and went back to her bedroom.

"Well, what do you know," said Mike.

Joshua and Zane had flown into Heathrow where they met and did a training course in forensics with the Metropolitan Police. Whilst there, they had permission from the government to see Deb to apologise that she had been framed.

It was 10:00 o'clock in the morning two weeks after they'd got back. Veronica picked up the phone which was ringing incessantly, "It's a phone call from the Chief Superintendent of the Metropolitan Police in London." Mike took the phone.

"Hello," he said, "how can I help you?"

The Superintendent explained that he had a couple of detectives with him from Bereithoa and they wanted to come down and talk to them all. They wouldn't need a solicitor or anything like that, it was just a chat and they just want to get a few things straight and straighten out a few things for them and especially Debbie. Would it be okay if the two detectives came over to see them that afternoon.

"Okay," Mike said.

They said they would arrive around about 2:30. The whole family would be there it was decided, to listen to what the two detectives had to say without committing themselves to anything and they could always consult with their solicitor later but Mike didn't want to spend any more money if they could help it and solicitors cost a lot.

At 2:30 the doorbell sounded and two men, Joshua and Zane, one about 6 feet 5 and the other one slightly shorter, were on the doorstep. Veronica let them in and made a coffee. They shook hands with everyone smiling and reassuringly introduced themselves and said that there was no problem with anything, but that they would like to update you on what has been happening.

"First of all, Debbie has been found not guilty now and this is a pardon from my government, and an apology that the investigation was not handled well at all."

He then handed over her personal belongings, passport etc It was a relief to get her belongings back.

"Your backpack's in the car," he said, "I will give you that later."

We have arrested certain people in the customs that were in on it and the Portuguese Police know who put the drugs into your bag. The only thing you are guilty of is leaving your bags with these people. The Spanish and Italian Police are currently investigating the drug gang, so we can say no more. We need to find them quickly, we have their contacts under arrest. There will not be any more drugs going through to South Africa from our country but I'm sure they will find another route so we need to get them. We have to.

He looked at Mike, smiled and said, "Sorry but you are not welcome in our country at all because everything you did was illegal and you shouldn't even have been in the country." He laughed.

"I'm not expecting you to want to go back to our country, even though it is beautiful – it is my home, both of our homes," Zane said, "We are the police there and we are not paid off by anyone. As far as Jack and your wife are concerned there's no evidence that they were ever in our country doing anything illegal so they're okay, it's just you."

"I hope I have put your minds at rest. It's not the first time we've met," he said to Debbie. "If you remember we were on the plane - or I was on the plane with my wife and children –

and you were playing with my children, keeping them occupied. I saw it was you who were arrested with your friends. I was sure that you were innocent but it takes time to get evidence."

"Thank you very much for seeing us" he added. "We will get going now, we were on a course here but we're finished now and on our way home. Goodbye."

They all shook hands and Debbie went out and collected her kit bag.

"Well, how about that," said Mike. "I'm the only one in the family with a police record."

~~~o~~~